MARGOT TENNEY

oode,

Merry Xmas
ave a successful
2006)
        Margot Tenney

Dar
Swe
A Jou

To Sh

and

year (

Dark Deeds, Sweet Songs

A Journal of Sorts

A Novel by

Margot Tenney

ARGONNE PUBLISHING INC.

DURHAM, NORTH CAROLINA

Published by
Argonne Publishing Inc.
Post Office Box 16030
Durham, North Carolina 27704

This book was printed on acid-free paper in the United States of America
and was composed by The Roberts Group.

Library of Congress Catalog Card Number: 94-71419

Dark Deeds, Sweet Songs:
A Journal of Sorts
by Margot Tenney

ISBN 0-9640152-0-X

10 9 8 7 6 5 4 3 2 1

First Edition and first book in a series introducing new authors

to Larry McBride and Amelia
in memoriam

Acknowledgments

↩ I would like to acknowledge and thank Laura Feigin, Lorenz Hansen, Bari Wood and Annouk Van de Voorde for their great help in minutely proofreading this novel. Ian Calderone, my patient friend, was always there for me. My dear husband, Del Tenney, was more than game, letting me expose his darker side without a whimper. He was a good sport during the long development of this story from journal entries to book.

With affection and devotion, I also would like to thank Charlotte Hoffman, my editor and publisher, who has taken the entire work through its many trying incarnations.

Last, I want to express my gratitude to the spirit of Collin, who enters my thoughts daily and reminds me of the depth and breadth of the word "giving."

MARGOT TENNEY
February 1995

Dark Deeds,
Sweet Songs

A Journal of Sorts

Entry One

The first thing I learned as an actress was how to die. At twelve years old, I was only playing at dying. I didn't find out the ugly realities for many years.

My group was studying with Ina Clark, a 52-year-old actress of the old school, who was preparing to play Lady Esplanade in *Never the Rose* at the Royal Theater in New York. She had been trained at the London Academy of Arts and Letters, where she received a gold medal for diction. She taught a stylized version of how to "act." Our classes were at the Riverside Church on the upper West Side. After school, three days a week, she demonstrated to our class of eight would-be actresses how to register shock and horror in the Bernhardt manner. The crowning achievement was to pass away on the floor like a diva, without bruising yourself.

The idea was to weave your way downward, imitating a cobra in reverse. Of course, there was the obligatory whimper, hand to temple, fluttering eyes that finally closed forever. Then, curtain.

We were at that awkward age and had a tendency to hit the floor like an upended tractor. I remember her saying to me, "Not like that, Blair, Darling. Die gracefully."

"Yes, Madam," I would reply, with respect.

Death scenes were my favorite. I could die a hundred different ways. I could stagger backward like the bad guy in western films, coughing my guts out because the bullet had hit me in the stomach, which I violently clutched. Then there was death à la Camille. I needed another actor to do that one. He had to pick up all 110 pounds of me and stagger over to a window so that I could deliver my heartrending farewell. I would bid him a wheezing goodbye with consumptive gasps before I let my arms and head go limp.

There was Madam Butterfly's hari-kari impersonation, and death in childbirth, the take-care-of-my-Ashley version. Death by poison, self-inflicted or otherwise, was as good as Tosca hurling herself off a parapet. All the scenes included a deathbed whisper or an appropriate shriek.

"I might have wanted to be a playwright, if I hadn't gotten the idea of becoming a stage actress first. The way people act both in plays and in real life intrigues me. I've decided all excitable behavior is a form of play-acting. I could go to the theater every day of the week."

That's what I wrote in my diary as a young girl. I dreamt of being on stage since the time my mother took me to see Wendy Hiller in *Pygmalion*.

But my favorite leading man was a motion picture actor. I'll improvise and re-create my feelings. ⌐

BLAIR: I am in love. I have fallen in love with Montgomery Clift. It was instant attraction. He is starring in *The Heiress* at the movie house on Eighty-sixth and Madison. Looking into his limpid eyes, up there on the big screen, I know he will be my heartthrob forever …"

⌐ It was love at first sight, although I had no idea then that he was gay and wouldn't have even known what that meant. I thought all sensitive men looked like Monty, if not as handsome, and I was going to marry someone just like him.

After seeing *The Heiress,* I felt certain that if only I were able to arrange a meeting with Monty on Beverly Glen Boulevard in Hollywood and bump into him by a brilliantly orchestrated maneuver I hadn't yet invented, he would see how clever and intoxicating I could be and naturally come to love me. That kind of thinking is probably why, up until a few years ago, I was still looking for those precious maneuvers to distract my husband from his Bambies and Muffies. My husband was different from Monty, but the charm was the same.

After I had starred in an original television drama for Alcoa Goodyear in New York the year I graduated from Bennington, I joined the Arena Theater in Washington, D.C., where I met

Leonard Stewart, an actor.

Our first production together was *Girl on the Via Flaminia,* and I was The Girl. Lisa. At last, I had an opportunity to die professionally and be paid for it. In this play I jumped off a bridge into some Roman river or other. Lisa killed herself for the love of a young soldier. He was played by Len, who had been trained in Hollywood. Our styles of acting were different. He didn't accept the long preparatory exercises that I found necessary to get into the mind of the character each evening before the play opened. ⌐

L E N : Why do you come to the theater so early?

B L A I R : It takes me an hour to do my hair and makeup and an hour to get into the part.

L E N : I don't go for that Stanislavsky shit. I just do deep breathing and imagine myself in Rome, lonely. In about fifteen minutes, I'm ready.

B L A I R : You're just playing *yourself.* My way is more difficult, Len, but more rewarding. I have to relive the whole life of an eighteen-year-old Italian girl who's far more insecure and desperate than I. I need time to imagine the sights and smells and dreadful things she feels, picture her poverty, feel the misery that drives her into prostitution. I can't do all that in fifteen minutes. I wouldn't believe it.

L E N : Why do you have to believe it? Say the lines and make the audience believe it.

BLAIR: That's cheating. Lisa wouldn't be real. She'd be shallow.

LEN: You're not paid to be real. You're paid to pretend.

BLAIR: I'm paid to be good. And so are you. If you think you can be a good actor after fifteen minutes, I don't! You Californians take too many shortcuts.

LEN: Actually, I was born in Iowa. Mother ran a chili restaurant there during the depression. Then she moved to California and opened a boutique. I worked my way through college doing construction, when I wasn't a baker, lumberman or gas station attendant. You name it. Perfect qualifications for acting.

BLAIR: How did you get into theater?

LEN: (*grins*) I was on the diving team in college. I was going to a swim meet with my friend Bill, an actor. We stopped at a theater where they were casting *Mister Roberts*. Bill urged me on. He said I was the type: clean-cut, honest-looking. Middle America. I auditioned for Ensign Pulver's part. They mistook me for an actor and I got it.

BLAIR: (*teasing*) Just as I thought. Everything comes without effort for you.

LEN: (*giving it right back*) And what about you? A pretty little Jewish-American princess, born with a silver spoon. It's a miracle you try so hard. On our farm in Iowa, we knew all about hard work. Not you.

BLAIR: (*passionately*) We can't pick how we're born. You

have to work hard to get anywhere. What are you going to do with this part of yours, anyway? Seems to me you're glossing over it, expecting the scenes just to pop into place.

LEN: If I felt I had to analyze every little nuance the way you do, I'd get out of the business. (*smiles, waves and exits*)

BLAIR: (*calls after him*) Theater's not business. It's art.

↩ Len and I began to enjoy our arguments, the jibing. We played young lovers in *Tartuffe* and Sean O'Casey's *Bedtime Story,* in addition to other roles. In less than a year, my Jewish-American father was walking me down the aisle to be Len's wife. My father had made a fortune in real estate. He was enraged that Len was an actor and had no money. He whispered, on the way to the rabbi, "You couldn't even marry a Jewish producer! I give it five years."

So Len and I were united, and I only hoped Daddy's prediction wouldn't come true. I was too naive to realize just how long five years could be. And how much a husband could change. ↩

Entry Two

↩ Five years later, Len and I had two children, were running an off-Broadway theater and still had very little money.

We ignored my father's deadline and decided to stay married.

Several years after that, catastrophe struck. Len thought he would follow my father's footsteps into real estate, which meant moving away from New York City. Len picked out Falls Village, Connecticut, where prices were affordable. To me, it was an exodus and an exile. I was devastated. I had to leave my parents, my friends, not to mention acting, the work and life I loved.

When I got pregnant, I had had to stop acting. But I picked it up again when the children were a few years older. It wasn't easy to convince directors I was serious after the time lapse. Following my husband to upstate Connecticut would kill my prospects. We were to move anyway. Serving what felt like a prelude to banishment, I plotted ways to return to the city, to tryouts, to agents, to a twenty-four-inch waistline, to Bergdorf's and Saks, to the museums, to cocktail parties, taxicabs, but mainly, to the hard work of a career that I had fantasized about since the sixth grade. I confronted Len in the sparsely furnished, small living room of our New York apartment, children in tow. I have to admit, ours was a handsome family. My son, Mark, took after me; our daughter, Kay, after Len. This is the way it went. ⤸

(Len, Kay *and* Mark *enter.*)

BLAIR: (*angrily*) I'm warning you, Darling. I don't want to move in the worst way, but I know how important it is to you to make more money. I realize our theater is going nowhere,

9

and real estate in the boonies sounds better right now. I'll have to put *my* career on hold. But don't ask me to stay longer than two years. Just two years, Len. If I hate living up there, we'll have to think of other options.

M A R K : I can't wait to go, Dad. The Indian Mountain School has a neat hockey team.

K A Y : Mommy, I'll have no one to play with. Let's you and I stay in New York.

L E N : Well, we certainly know whose daughter *she* is. (*kneels and caresses his daughter*) Think how happy your kitty will be up there. And the dog, too. Honey, we can all go horseback riding and boating and take long walks through the woods together.

K A Y : (*pulls away and starts to whimper*) I'm scared of horses. Mommy and I will get lost in the woods. Or fall out of the boat and drown.

B L A I R : Mark, take Kay into the dining room. Your dinners are getting cold. (*The children depart. She calls after them.*) I promise you, Kay, we won't have to stay there more than a year or two. (*turns to Len*) Honestly, Leonard, swear that this is just a trial … We could compromise and move to Stamford or Greenwich and be only an hour out of New York.

L E N : I can't afford property in Greenwich or Stamford. Upstate, costs are less than half. I predict you'll get used to Falls Village, Blair. You'll see. You and Kay and Mark will make new friends, and we'll all be so healthy we'll live forever.

BLAIR: I'm not so sure I wouldn't rather die a little earlier, here.

LEN: Two years, Blair. That's all I ask.

BLAIR: (*looking at him meaningfully*) All right. As long as you behave yourself. You get my meaning?

LEN: You haven't a thing to worry about. All that is over. Especially if you concentrate on our family, stop running around to auditions and taking parts. (*exits*)

↶ So, we departed for Connecticut and Kay was right, there was no one to play with. No close friend to make me feel valued. You can't make your husband and children your whole life. At least, I couldn't. If I wasn't going to be doing something in theater, at least I had to be doing *something*. The days seemed endless while the children were in school, and Leonard kept working long hours. Each day seemed a repetition of the dull one before it.

Alone one of those many gray days in Falls Village, I wrote in my journal:

"From concrete I rose and under concrete I hope to return—if not alive, at least to be buried someday in New York City. I would be delighted if someone could just find a way to dispose of my ashes under one of those rusty pothole covers, let's say, in the theater district, or perhaps under Fifty-seventh Street, not far from the Russian Tea Room's red canopy. Better yet, let my ashes drift over Fifth and Fifty-ninth, to be happily stomped under the feet of those fat, hairy horses resting by the curb, heads nuzzled in their feed bags, waiting to draw tourist carriages, reeking deliciously of sweat and city grime. New York is the city I will want to see out my window when I am sucking in my last breath."

That about covers my state of mind when I met Collin Williams. He, Leonard and I play the leads in my journal. What I didn't realize at the time was that for the next twenty years, I was going to be living with two men. ᕫ

Entry Three

ᕫ So it was to Falls Village, in the township of Lakeville, in Litchfield County, Connecticut, we had moved. I was no longer a New Yorker, and my husband was no longer Len. He had passed the nickname stage, at least he thought he had. After we were in this new full-time home for a few months, it became apparent to me, though not to Leonard, that I had never really comprehended the word "imprisoned" before.

There was the house surrounded by trees and a road, and that road was forty-five minutes from the nearest train station, from which point the train took another two hours to get to New York. Because of the traffic approaching the city, driving there was worse. I missed the people-to-people cluttered sidewalks. Why, there were more daisies in the fields than there were people in the whole town of Falls Village and neighboring Lime Rock put together. Furthermore, I hadn't been able to find anyone to help me up in the middle of nowhere, and Mark and Kay, eight and seven respectively, were banging in and out the screen door with newfound rambunctiousness. All that energy must have been pumped into their lungs along with the invigorating, pollen-infested air.

I thought of the fragrance of Wendy Hiller's flowers in *Pygmalion*. The sweetness of the scent had made me dizzy. It overwhelmed me, and I thought, as I breathed in, that it was better than all those countryside wildflowers Mother insisted we stop and smell in the fields behind the Barrows Hotel in Cedarhurst, Long Island. My parents used to take me there on weekends when I was a kid. An only child—unfortunately—I found the country a lonely place. There had been no one to play with at the Barrows, either. Every few weeks, we drove across the Whitestone Bridge, and I would feel my heart sink into that murky water where tugboats deposited stinking oil. That damned bridge took me away from New York.

Daddy drove us, Mother sitting passively beside him. In those days, I guess, women never drove. Daddy said we were supposed to fill our lungs with "the great outdoors." He was a killer about the great outdoors. And he was just as bad in the winter, when he used to wake me up on weekends and send me downstairs, down six flights at 8:30 on a Saturday morning, to get that loathsome fresh air! I couldn't wait to get back upstairs.

I hated the idea of fresh air even worse in Falls Village. Unlike my children, no vigor infused *my* being. I rarely budged from the Falls Village house except to do grocery shopping or to get this and that from the hardware store. It seemed everything in our house needed fixing.

Gradually, I settled into a morass. Way out on that dusty, remote country road, I was alone most of the time. It wasn't hard to imagine that Leonard, with his new Connecticut real estate license burning a hot spot in the pocket of his tweed jacket, had enough time on his hands to do some real damage. I figured he would soon be on the prowl again. All it would take was an admiring smile from someone named Binky or Muffy or Bambi from this WASP-ish countryside. The lank-haired ladies took a liking to sandy-haired Leonard—with his wide hazel eyes and ready smile—and they all had something in common: they were young and in need of recreational sex, and Leonard, who *wasn't* in need, thought it all a game.

My father had warned, "Never marry an actor!" But who listens to a parent when she's twenty-three and has hot pants? To me, Leonard had had one especially irresistible feature. He was far from being the dictatorial German-Jewish-Austrian that Daddy was. As Leonard immersed himself in real estate, they began to seem more alike.

One late afternoon—May, I think it was—I felt particularly depressed. A fox had crept out of the woods and gobbled up the cat, Mitzu. Or so I supposed. Mitzu had disappeared, and our nearest neighbor said there was a fox in the field behind our house.

My poor city cat. I believed *we,* at least, would be safe in this quaint, if confusing, hamlet. Our zip code was based in Canaan, our mail was sent to Falls Village, and our telephone number was a Lakeville exchange. Falls Village was also a strange place socially. A lot of dropouts lived there, including young men with nasty-looking, scraggly beards. Not the picturesque Greenwich Village kind I was used to.

Plenty of farmers and struggling artists lived in Falls Village. I tried to make friends with their wives. When I went to Bud's Market in town, with Mark and Kay, we all were delighted with the display of country wares. There were small baskets filled with penny candy on the counter. Larger baskets contained gorgeous, shiny red crab apples. There were handmade dolls and hand-carved wooden toy boats among the many rows of canned goods on the shelves. They sold everything in that store. Car oil and ice-cream makers and butter churns, hammers, traps for rodents, fire wood and pool chemicals. It was a circus of color and scents. The smell of spices made me ravenous. I bought things to eat that nobody wanted when I got home.

Bud was distant but friendly. ↩

BLAIR: Thanks for sending someone to fix the septic tank, Bud. What do I owe you?

B U D : (*chuckles, embarrassed*) I'll work that out with Len.

B L A I R : (*reaches inside* her *handbag*) I'd rather write you the check right now.

B U D : I'll send the bill to Len's office.

B L A I R : I have an idea. Why don't you and your wife stop by Saturday afternoon with the children and have lunch? We can take care of it then. The kids can play together.

B U D ' S W I F E : (*stands at the cash register*) Kids got chores on Saturdays, Miz Stewart. Farm children don't go running around visiting, like city children.

B L A I R : (*too eagerly*) Oh, that's what my husband says. He was raised on a farm. What about dinner? You could come at six, or seven, after the … uh, chores.

B U D ' S W I F E : We got a big family to worry about; we don't rightly go out Saturday nights. The old folks live with us, and I gotta feed Grandpa Hayes real early.

B L A I R : (*desperately*) Well … what about Sunday, after church? …

M A R K : (*comes up and grabs her arm, whispers vehemently*) Mother, shut up! She doesn't want to. *Nobody* wants to visit you.

B L A I R : (*puts her finger to her lips and tries to smile*) Hush, Mark! (*to* Bud's *wife*) Maybe some other time … Where on earth did you buy that magnificent handmade sweater?

B U D ' S W I F E : Sweater? (*looks down as if she'd forgotten what she'd put on*)

BLAIR: Does a local shop sell them? Is it mail order? I'd love to buy one.

BUD'S WIFE: Miz Stewart, around these parts we knit our own. I unraveled an afghan to make this. Moths had got into it. Guess you didn't knit in New York. We heard you were (*pauses disapprovingly*) ... We heard you were on the *stage.*

KAY: (*jumps right in*) She was, but Daddy won't let her anymore. She did one whole scene in her slip in front of hundreds of people.

BUD'S WIFE: Dear Lord.

BLAIR: (*firmly, hastily*) Mark and Kay, we are leaving right this minute. Come along.

BUD: You just tell Len not to worry about that bill. I'll catch up with him at the real estate office.

∽ Few of the local wives ever accepted my invitations. Finally, I found out that the way to start a conversation in Falls Village was to talk about the weather. Everyone spoke of the weather with rare delight, becoming animated about the rise in water level on the banks of the Housatonic when a full moon was on the way. I never even *saw* the moon in New York. We were considered New Yorkers from the day we arrived. We were outsiders until we sold our first place, and only then was it referred to as the Stewart farm.

The Bloods, who did become friends, were prominent in town. Jake, the old man, pushed soil and buildings around with a heavy-duty bulldozer. He looked like God molding the firmament, sitting up on high, waving down at us amiably. Len gave him remodeling work, and he appeared to like us. Even so, he commented on our ways. The butcher at the local country market said Jake called us "the weird guys—nice, but weird." I bumped into him when I was buying an ice cream maker one day. He shook his head and said that his wife was still using a churn you primed with good old rock salt.

Differences in my lifestyle and those of the other residents got to me. I had the children and a household to run, of course. But what was I to think about, to plan and dream about, with the theater 120 miles away? I tried to be open, to express my feelings. ⌐

B L A I R : I can't understand it, Leonard.

L E O N A R D : (*sits, looking at some papers*) Understand what?

B L A I R : How the hell you went into real estate when theater was our whole life. The theater is what drew us together. Now, we hardly have anything to talk about. What do I care that you sold the Morgan house or that they're changing the zoning on Elm Street? I feel as if I'm just drifting, with no goal in sight. I need your enthusiasm to inspire me. But it's focused elsewhere.

L E O N A R D : I have to get ahead in the world, Blair. I want the respect that comes with that. Try to pull yourself together and broaden your horizons. You think things were going so well in New York? We were broke, living on doles from your father in five dark little rooms, with even more roaches than unpaid bills. You think that was class? You wanna go back to that? Be my guest.

BLAIR: (*heatedly*) Our lives could have been worse. We cared about the same things there.

LEONARD: You forget how self-absorbed you were in New York. Total immersion in some play or audition. (*mimics her*) "How do I *look*? How do I *sound*? Oh, not now. I don't have *time*" … Not for us, not for anything but your own artsy-fartsy daydreams.

BLAIR: What are you talking about? You were the producer and director of your own theater. I was only an actress. You never even *paid* me. I hired an au pair with money from my parents to perform in your plays. You agreed. You have a hell of a nerve to complain now. Besides, a lot of women work. Why shouldn't I?

LEONARD: Most women come home and leave their work behind. They make time for their husbands. Not my Blair. I could see it in your eyes, always thinking about your part. I'd talk about my problems and you'd be absentmindedly fingering your script. Only the character you were playing was real. You, Blair Stewart, weren't really there with me.

BLAIR: (*bitterly*) You never suffered long. Always some bimbo waiting in the wings to soothe poor Leonard, whose wife doesn't have time for him.

LEONARD: I'm surprised you even noticed.

BLAIR: That's not fair. You *married* an actress. If you

hadn't become disenchanted, stopped the creative life yourself, you would be more understanding of me. But you just got up and ran. You weren't committed. Changed professions, demanded we leave town when you wanted. I should have known better. My father was right.

LEONARD: It's fine to do what you want, but survival comes first.

BLAIR: You were beginning to make it. *Two* film offers. You could have hung in longer.

LEONARD: Bullshit. At least give me credit for trying something else. Real estate in Connecticut was good enough for your father. It put him on Fifth Avenue and got you through Bennington. And stop kidding yourself about how good you had it in New York. Have you forgotten those fights about money? Up here, I can afford to support our family without handouts from your parents.

BLAIR: (*close to tears*) And what about my feelings? I don't fit in here.

LEONARD: You have the kids. Why not try to find yourself some friends through them? Get active at their school.

BLAIR: The PTA is just like the other groups. I go and sit alone. Oh, Leonard, if you only would understand just how unhappy …

LEONARD: (*exasperated*) So join something else. Get a part-time job. Teach a course. *Take* a course. How the hell should I know? (*grabs his work and storms out*)

⌐ I was brooding about what Leonard had said one rainy afternoon in May, when I saw Collin Williams walking down the road. ⌐

 *Entry Four*

⌐ All week, the weather had been damp, even for spring. I lit the logs in the fireplace (after the fifth try), and, while I was staring into the fire, longing for the taste of a cafe espresso at the Russian Tea Room, I prayed for something, *anything,* to happen. The flames licked and spit and I saw the face of Satan in that tiny blaze. I called out to him. I offered him my soul in exchange for the prospect of a little excitement, a happening of any kind, the entrance of anyone in pretty clothes; or, barring that, the entrance of anyone capable of laughter.

I had been accustomed to going to the theater or to films in the city on bleak, gray afternoons—not to feeling abandoned, left to stare at a few weak flames and then out the window at the woods.

As I waited for Leonard to come home, I thought of poets I had read in college. They were the only ones I could think of who might appreciate this gloom. A line from Gray's *Elegy* came to mind: "And leaves the world to darkness and to me."

What an alarming prospect! It would soon be the witching hour. Leonard would probably be late again, and the children had gone to a birthday party. I'd have given anything for someone to be there with me.

The devil must have been listening: I wouldn't be left alone much longer. I believe now that what the devil decided to do was to take my soul and give me Collin Williams in its place. A person appeared down the road's gloomy corridor. There he was, a tiny, bouncing, promising speck, off in the distance. Coming toward me!

As he drew nearer, I saw that he was tall and much absorbed in the pleasure of his own thoughts. He looked as if he hardly knew it was raining! Where could he be headed, I wondered? Our house was sandwiched in between Hezzy Raymond's fields and the river. Hezzy (the game warden and land-poor dairy farmer), like Leonard, was rarely home.

I peered through the drizzle. The stranger was quite close now. Calling him skinny would have been an understatement. There he came, grinning, meandering, looking up at the sky, at the rain, as if all of nature were shining.

Happily, catching his mood, I grabbed my jacket and fled the empty house.

In the driveway, I hesitated, stopped and held my breath. This man appeared to be the village idiot, a walking scarecrow. Whatever he was, he seemed delighted to see me. I decided, judging by his shy smile, that he wasn't a murderer or rapist.

Besides, I recalled that old Mrs. Williams lived on Hezzy's land, behind the woods. I had heard that she and her husband were tenant farmers, with two grown sons and a daughter, who had run away. It seemed entirely possible that this sky watcher, this damp-day walker, was one of their sons. One more of the country boys who populated this corner of Litchfield, where the Riley kid was soon to be accused of murdering his mother on a nearby farm.

When I first spied Collin, he looked very much like I imagined Aaron Slick from Punkin Crick, the character in an old melodrama. To be more flattering, I could describe Collin as a man with a hesitant manner. Much later, in his middle forties, he would become more gaunt and color his hair, which thinned considerably, so much so that he wore a black Greek sailor's cap almost all the time. But when we met, he had dark hair brushed sideways, touching the top of his ears, and long on his neck. Collin's skin was pocked and craggy, and there was a childlike openness about him. He stood and waited.

I spoke first. ⮑

BLAIR: Hello. I see you're out for a stroll. Such pretty flowers you have there.

COLLIN: It's amazing. The crocuses are really yellow this year. I walked all the way up from Mrs. Marlin's. She's got loads of them along the stream by the old forge. I don't mind walking. Any kind of travel will do. See, I take a shortcut around

Hezzy's pond, then skirt the racetrack. Sometimes, I go clear over to Route 112. Now, if you take …

BLAIR: (*smiling*) You're a walking road map, aren't you?

COLLIN: (*smiles sheepishly*) … Oh, my mother always tells me that. A habit, I guess. I've got a book on every boat that has ever sailed and every train … well … Here! Flowers that bloom in May / brighten up a rainy day. (*chuckles*) I always like the poetry on greeting cards. Sometimes, I try to write that stuff myself. (*stretches out the little bouquet in her direction*) You can have them.

BLAIR: (*takes flowers*) Oh, how nice! The rain did make me feel kind of low. These'll pick up my spirits. Even better than martinis at the Carlisle.

COLLIN: On Madison Avenue, in New York. Three blocks up from St. James Church.

BLAIR: (*amazed*) You know the city?

COLLIN: I take the train to New York whenever I can. I'm big on cathedrals. I also read a lot. Collin Williams' my name. Collin, with two "els." (*extends his hand*) I live with my mother and brother. Over there.

BLAIR: Hello, Collin. I'm Blair, with one "el." Blair Stewart.

COLLIN: (*looks around curiously*) You're doing a lot of construction.

BLAIR: (*sighs*) Yes, we're buying old houses, remodeling and selling. Sometimes we add a wing, if the location's good. Real estate is what brought us to Falls Village. At least, it brought my husband. To him, carpentry and the smell of wood is an aphrodisiac.

COLLIN: I don't like the smell of wood. My mother used to tie me to a tree when I was little.

BLAIR: How terrible!

COLLIN: (*shrugs*) Women do that. Can't afford baby-sitters, I guess. (*smiles*) I like the feel of wood, though.

BLAIR: Is your father living?

COLLIN: He's in a convalescent home in Torrington. He used to farm. Mom's on welfare now. Hezzy makes plenty of money off people like her. She's old. My brother's a drinker. He doesn't work, most of the time. It makes me mad.

BLAIR: So you're the only one in your family who's working?

COLLIN: That's right. (*proudly*) I've never been on welfare. I often stay over at Mrs. Marlin's. The lady with the pointed feather in her hat? Real estate broker. I help her redo old houses, like you.

BLAIR: Would you come in for a cup of tea?

COLLIN: Yeah, sure. (*They go inside the house. He points to the crocuses* Blair *is holding.*) Have you noticed what a wonderful shade those are? Three years ago, they were much lighter. When you don't drive, you walk a lot. You notice the changes.

BLAIR: Collin, this is the first time I've lived in rural America. Being a native New Yorker, I haven't learned to distinguish the colors of flowers.

COLLIN: (*sympathetically*) Too bad. That's what life's all about. (*He joins her at the table and sits.*) Nature is for people who feel, / nothing else is truly real.

👈 I realized later that Collin always took time to chat with any stranger he met. This abject friendliness would someday make him a mark. That day, I picked up on it with open arms. Frankly, he could have been barking like a dog; he was what I had yearned for ... someone to talk to.

We sat together at the kitchen table, and I asked Collin about his life. 👈

BLAIR: What did you do for a living, Collin? Before you met Mrs. Marlin.

COLLIN: I was a painter.

BLAIR: Wonderful! Impressionistic, abstract, realistic? Let me guess. The way you love flowers, you were a landscape artist. (*gets up to pour hot water from the teakettle into their cups*)

COLLIN: (*shyly*) I wouldn't say I was an artist.

BLAIR: So modest. Do you prefer oil or watercolors?

COLLIN: (*accepts cup of tea*) Thank you. I use oil on exteriors. Some folks like water-base paint, but I don't think you can beat oil.

BLAIR: Do you use brushes or a palette knife?

COLLIN: Brush for trim, but a roller covers walls faster.

BLAIR: Wait a minute. You paint murals on walls?

COLLIN: I paint *walls*. And exteriors too, weather permitting.

BLAIR: (*embarrassed*) Oh, of course. I was thinking of museums. City girl, remember? Different frame of reference. Don't mind me, Collin. Let me know when you're ready for more tea.

⤿ Collin sipped his tea and became quiet. It was an amiable if addled silence, after such repartee. You lunatic, I thought. Can't you understand this man comes from a world with a different language than yours? Yet there were similarities. Some Falls Villagers walked everywhere, like people in New York. They couldn't drive because they couldn't afford cars. Certainly not Collin's family. I supposed that, like so many of the long-term inhabitants, his ancestors had been smelters on Mount Riga. There still was a colony of them up on the mountain, even though iron smelting was no longer a local trade. The era of the train had long since come to an end; most of the descendants had moved to the lowlands and become tenant farmers. They were still referred to as "raggies."

Our backgrounds and expectations were as different as cobalt blue and Dutch Boy red. Collin and I had many conversations like the first. Our perceptions sailed past each other. Often, I didn't understand what he meant. I was never quite sure whether Collin was an artless innocent, or indeed the devil for whom I had exchanged my soul. ⤿

Entry Five

⌐ Collin cared too much about what people thought of him. Some people do, you know. My mother did. And like my mother, Collin always worried. You could tell by the way he dressed, with that English pipe hanging from his mouth, like Sherlock Holmes. And whenever the pipe went out, he always kept his mouth closed. That's because he didn't want people to see his bad teeth. Mother understood that about him. She understood all about appearances.

One weekend, when Mother came to visit us in Falls Village, she gave Collin the money for a set of false teeth. When he got them, he had to relearn how to eat corn on the cob. He was embarrassed about that. Yet he had needed the bridgework. Mother saw that right after she met him. She understood why he never opened his mouth to smile. She and Collin had vanity in common. Both were equally mortified: she, much later, when she lost her hair after chemotherapy; he, after losing his front teeth. Her gift cured his problem. There would be no cure for hers.

The day after our tea party, I introduced Collin to Leonard. Leonard asked him to do several jobs. He did many. I observed, as the months went by, that Collin was often forgetful. It occurred to me that he might be what they call neurologically impaired. But what would you expect, with a mother like his? Probably left him tied to that tree too long! Despite his early abuse, he was good with the children. Mark and Kay tolerated him better than they had the au pair in New York.

I thought it strange, but not insurmountable, that Collin's reactions were slow. I figured that this was partly because of his lack of education. He admitted he hadn't gotten past the sixth grade. But it made no difference to me then that there was something a little odd about him. Suddenly, some word or idea he expressed would appear out of nowhere. Yet, his vagueness and slowness was offset by an incredible kindness.

Soon Collin was living with us. He loved elegant cars and became enthralled with our Bentley. Leonard taught him to drive, never yelling or bracing himself against the dashboard, the way my father would have. Collin moved into an apartment over the garage he and Leonard built, quit his job with Mrs. Marlin and worked for us exclusively. His chores were gardening, helping me in the house, helping prepare the meals and doing heavy cleaning. He baby-sat the children when I went into New York overnight, to see my parents.

He and I were busiest in the garden. He taught me how to grow vegetables, as well as flowers. ⇐

COLLIN: Those carrots of yours look sick. Jagged, uneven.

BLAIR: (*annoyed*) I don't plant carrots to look pretty. I plant them to eat.

COLLIN: You don't have the right idea at all. Everything in life should be filled with grace, / what's wrong with your scowling … look? expression? no, *face*. How can you plant without joy?

BLAIR: There's no joy in listening to your idiotic rhymes. And stop *trying* to make me smile. I'm hot and smelly and tired.

COLLIN: You could pretend this is an acting improvisation. Did I say that right?

BLAIR: (*laughs, in spite of herself*) You sure as hell did, and I wish it were.

✍ Collin and I talked a lot about flowers and recipes and about what we read in the newspapers. He began borrowing my books, and I was surprised at the depth with which he discussed the people he read about. Mountbatten was one of his favorites. The history of countries sent him into ecstasy. He haunted secondhand bookstores on his days off and brought home every conceivable biography, as well as books about planes, trains and ships.

In fact, Collin collected just about everything. That drove me crazy. He saved his money, and when he had made exactly the right amount to the penny, he packed up and left for a trip. Never any warning. One day there; the next, his suitcase was missing and his door locked. What did he have to hide? I was to find out later.

He went to Europe and traveled his heart out, often to France, about which he talked constantly.

We were in the kitchen. I was sewing, Collin was washing dishes. ∽

BLAIR: Well, so you're leaving again, Collin. Off to Paris to devour soufflés.

COLLIN: I got my francs and centimes from the Thomas Cook Agency. *Au revoir* now. See you in ten days. *Bonne chance.*

BLAIR: *Bonne chance,* and *merci* to you, Collin. *Au revoir* as well.

COLLIN: (*beside himself*) Would you mind repeating that? I love the way your voice sounds when you speak French. *Au revoir, au revoir.* A *votre santé, à bientôt.* I'll try to learn a few more phrases before I get back. Spending my money will not be in vain, / as long as I can boat down the Seine. Ah, the *bateaux mouche!*

BLAIR: I'm sure France will be worth the expense.

∽ Then, with tenderness, I would tell him, "*Au revoir,* Collin," again. That simple phrase could send him into a swoon that lasted through the bed making, the errands, the floor washing, right up till his early afternoon detailed reading of the *Enquirer.*

When Collin returned from his trips, we'd talk about every

moment he'd spent walking the streets of Paris, staying on the Left Bank, where one particular concierge knew him by name. Collin knew the detailed route the metro took to Versailles and where in town was every *eglise*. He knew the history of churches; he memorized the menus in every restaurant that charged under twenty francs. ✍

(Collin *enters and sits at the table.* Blair *joins him. They are shelling peas.*)

COLLIN: (*painfully, carefully splitting open the pods*) The place to stay in Paris is a little pension on the Left Bank. The owners know me well by now, of course. They always find me a wonderful room. Once, I told Mrs. Marlin about it. Mrs. Marlin and I share an interest in traveling. She used to go at night to the remotest places in strange countries and not even get nervous. In Mexico, she went by herself to a cockfight after midnight.

BLAIR: Most women that age take tours. It's safer. She has guts. You do too, Collin. It's amazing the way you go all over. And figure out foreign currencies, or when trains leave and for where.

COLLIN: (*beams*) It's easy ... if you plan. I plan down to my last nickel. Upstairs I have all the updated plane and train schedules. The travel agents give them to me. And when I get where I'm going, I walk the streets for hours ... really get to know the town. And you gotta talk to everybody. And I do!

BLAIR: (*smiles*) Oh, I'm sure you do. You like to talk to

people. Especially old ladies. That's why you like ship travel, I suppose.

COLLIN: I know the layout of every ship sailing. I'm going to be buried at sea, you know. In my next reincarnation, I'll be a sea captain.

BLAIR: Why do you say that?

COLLIN: An astrologer in New York told me so. You know that actor friend of Leonard's? That Jeremiah? Well, he did my chart. I believe him. He tells me I'm going to take many more journeys. You know, I can ride out storms in a ship and never get sick at all.

BLAIR: And you flirt with all the nice old dowagers. (*teasing*) I'll bet you could find a wife that way, Collin.

COLLIN: (*deadly serious*) I just might. I like older ladies. I correspond with some of them, you know. They tell me about their gardens and their grandchildren.

BLAIR: And what do you tell them?

COLLIN: About *our* garden. About some of those crazy outfits you buy and all the places I drive you to. The theater, the airports. The Lawn and Tennis Club in New Haven, your parents' beach house.

BLAIR: And they're interested?

COLLIN: Sure, I tell them all about you. About all the interesting friends you made in the theater, and about the celebrities you have over sometimes. About your New York friends. They like to hear all that.

BLAIR: And do you tell them you won't call me Mrs.

33

Stewart or Blair? You call Leonard, Leonard, but you call me, Lady. (*She teases, imitates him.*) "Lady, you don't plant cucumbers that way." "Lady ... you back up hills like this." Or ... "Lady, are you home? ... telephone!" Sounds like you're calling the dog. "Here, Lady!"

COLLIN: Come on, now! NO, I don't tell them that. Besides, you named the dog Ophelia.

BLAIR: Don't be so literal. Just how do you describe your job, Collin?

COLLIN: Oh, I tell people I'm a caretaker. I tell them you and Leonard couldn't do without me. I tell them I'm a cook and chauffeur and gardener. And plug fixer, china gluer. I tell them Leonard goes away on business—that he may even get his own plane. So I sort of ... sort of take his place. I tell them I do a little of just about everything around here.

BLAIR: (*laughs*) God knows WHAT they think you mean by that!

COLLIN: (*preening*) Yeah. Well, whatever they want to believe ... Let them. I don't care. I don't mind.

BLAIR: (*softly*) You like being a member of the family, don't you, Collin?

COLLIN: Well, I'm not a servant.

BLAIR: No one ever called you that. (*thinks a bit*) But what are you, then?

COLLIN: (*contemplates*) I suppose I'm a friend.

(Collin *exits*. Leonard *enters*.)

BLAIR: Leonard! Back again. What is it, Darling?

LEONARD: The prospect phoned. Our appointment's canceled. So, here I am.

BLAIR: Come sit down and talk to me. What do you think about Collin referring to himself as our friend?

LEONARD: True, from his viewpoint. You always thought he was. And, since he's been with us, you're almost yourself again, so I'm grateful. But deep down, I feel he doesn't care about us or anyone. He simply knows how to survive, like a cat. As for his peculiar behavior—well, you get used to that. In fact, after a while, I hardly notice. But I don't care for the fact that he can be an awful squealer, when he wants to get your attention.

BLAIR: You don't like his squealing on you.

LEONARD: He keeps track of my goings and comings. He tells you every little move I make.

BLAIR: What's wrong about that, if you have nothing to hide? Besides, he's good company when you're gone, Leonard.

LEONARD: (*huffy*) When am I gone?

BLAIR: Gone? You come and go all the time. Whenever you want. When you're in town, you pop in anytime. Then you disappear somewhere like Rhode Island, and I can't even reach you by phone. Sometimes, I wonder whether you're coming back.

LEONARD: I'm looking at property in Rhode Island, working for *us,* you know! The more time I spend at work, the more suspicious you get. The only-child syndrome. Possessive, worried you're losing something. You want all the attention. ALL THE TIME. I suppose moving away from your parents and

35

friends and the theater was hard. But I can't make up my mind which is worse, your total involvement when you are in theater or your anger, thinking that I've pulled you away from it ... (*exits*)

BLAIR: (*watches him go*) So many faults, and all of them mine. What about *him?* When Leonard gets moody, he won't say what's wrong. He just sits and glowers and won't answer me. I'm just glad I have Collin to count on. So far, they haven't both taken off and left me at the same time—or for the same reasons. Sometimes I believe Collin cares for me more than Leonard does.

 Entry Six

I flipped through the diary of an earlier, more ingenious period of my life. I read aloud the text of the stained, blue-penned scribbles: memoirs of a girl's youth and dreams. So tentative, this writing. Unsure, I'd call it. I ask myself who *was* that girl? I have to go back to the years before Leonard to understand the needy creature I had been, to know who that character Blair, daughter of Joe and Dot Neville, really was.

In those days, life was gentle because I was living on Fifth Avenue and my parents' servants, Anna and Oscar, had just entered the scene.

Still, discord was sometimes present. Oscar battled and vacuumed while Anna cooked and complained, and my parents fought as well, though we had it easier than most. My parents admired Anna and Oscar because they worked very hard and saved their money. They dreamed of returning to Italy and opening a restaurant. They had learned to cook German food for my father, and in Italy that would be a specialty.

Oscar drove Daddy to work each day in Stamford, handled the heavy cleaning and took care of the yard at the house in Atlantic Beach. Anna cooked, kept house and did the laundry. They were short; Anna was plump and he, muscular and wiry. They were working in a small trattoria outside Portofino when my parents met them on one of their trips. My father offered them a job on the spot.

One day, Oscar and I, in my early teens, were washing my father's car. ✍

BLAIR: Oscar, when Daddy taught you to drive, he must have made you crazy. The way he slammed his foot down every time you went near the expressway ramp. How he braced himself against the dashboard, screaming at you to slow down, with that look on his face.

OSCAR: (*shakes his head*) I only go twenty miles an hour. Almost standing still. So many times I come close to big accident with him. His nerves give me nerves. Driving in New York City is bad.

BLAIR: What's the traffic like in Rome?

OSCAR: We didn't live in Roma. One day, little Blair. One day we go back and live in Roma.

BLAIR: What's my father like to work for, Oscar? He has such a temper.

OSCAR: I understand that kind of temper. He is like an Italian. An explosion, then *molto calmo*. He is a strong man. He takes care of you and your mother. Your mother is a very gentle soul, Blair. She needs protection.

BLAIR: Does she tell you all the time what to do, like she does me? Come home early, lower your voice, hang up your clothes. Do this, don't do that. Does she?

OSCAR: The signora is a lady. Anna and I like to please her. Ah, but your father, he is the big boss. Now, shoot the hose over here where I have put the soap.

↩ Oscar and Anna were secretive enough for us not to know what they really thought. As the years went by, God knows what they said behind our backs. It became obvious that they had respect only for my father.

Anyway, when I was a teenager, with Mother's couple to take care of us, I was free to dream. I fantasized I would have a future as an actress. A fairy-tale life of my own making. I thought everything would go right, because I felt sure I was in complete control of my own destiny. I worked and studied hard, people sometimes said I was beautiful, and why wouldn't things go my way?

It was just a dream, after all.

While Daddy drove us out to Barrows in Cedarhurst, in my mind, I acted out every role I ever played in school, including the Virgin Mary in the Christmas pageant. I pictured myself holding baby Jesus in my arms, wondering why my Christian classmates had voted for me, a Jewish girl, to play the Virgin. I suppose it was because they had decided the actors would speak lines from the Bible that year, and I was the best actress in the class, thanks to Madame Clark. As I sat in the car, I relived the rehearsals, the excitement of days of preparation in the big auditorium, where I would soon be receiving a diploma from Dalton, at my eighth-grade graduation. My parents, as usual, expected me to be outstanding. There was no room in their lives for a daughter who was less than exemplary.

My father was a very blunt man, a bit violent, and I thought most men were scary, if my father was an example. I actually was afraid of men and their mysterious ways. I attributed maleness to an aberration of chromosomes, and I wasn't eager to acquiesce to their demands. Playing the Virgin Mary must have affected me. I stayed a virgin long after most of my friends had labeled virginity "outré."

Virginity, however, didn't stop romantic dreams from haunting my sleep. I continually dreamed about the sexual encounter that would bring on the fabled explosion. I knew it had to happen: the movies told me so. I was Every Girl, and Every Man was out there somewhere. They all couldn't be like my father.

My friends talked endlessly about the great Love

happening—love with a capital "el," with its pelvic thrusts and tremblings and its ever-afters. In novels, we read about the assumption that God created women to fall in love with men. First, we were supposed to be delicate flowers; pelvic thrusts would come later. This romantic love that I read so much about would make me glad I had waited so patiently. And, of course, there was no doubt in my mind that he, who was on his way, would worship me.

By thirteen, I had already completed my first year of acting and felt talent exuding from me. My instructors agreed with this self-evaluation, so I was convinced. I would become an acclaimed actress, shining up there on stage in a halo of light. I threw myself into the part of Mary. You never knew who might be in the audience.

My cousin Joanie had little respect for my passion. ⬅

JOANIE: I never saw anyone rehearse as long as you. Why can't you just wing it? Why can't we go down and look at the tree in Rockefeller Plaza? Why must you hole away here and study, when you only have ten lines? We don't even believe in the New Testament.

BLAIR: It's the beginning of my career, Joanie. I gotta get her reactions right. I want the audience to see the premonition of Jesus' death on His mother's face. I don't want to be just okay as Mary. I want to make her come to life.

JOANIE: No one really cares. All you need to do is put on the costume, hold the baby, and not fall off the stage.

BLAIR: I want more than that. Go on, leave. I've got another hour of improvisation.

JOANIE: What the hell is that?

BLAIR: It's when you create a scene from your own life that makes you feel what the character in the play is feeling.

JOANIE: How can you invent having a baby, when you've never even been to bed with a man?

BLAIR: Your mind's on one thing only! No, Joanie, I'm looking for the feeling of joy, of reverence for new life. Like when Daddy gave me a puppy and I knew it was mine to love and take care of. I want to reinvent that feeling.

JOANIE: Muffin got run over. Bad things happened to your dog.

BLAIR: Bad things happened to Jesus, too.

⌐ I was secretly hoping I'd impress that Episcopalian dreamboat from Horace Mann with my performance. Surely, *he* believed in the New Testament. Would he be at the theater the night of the Christmas pageant, and would he ever call me?

Glancing back at the entries, I saw that my teenage diary was riddled with speculation: "Why did he's?" and "Why couldn't he have's?" and "Why didn't I have the courage to's?" It's sad really, because as I read on, it seemed to contain pages filled with self-doubt and "might have been's."

When I married Leonard, after the children were born, after romance turned bloody and a bit nasty, after a fox came out of Hezzy's woods and ate my cat, and after life pitched its usual

41

low balls, the tone of my journal changed. In fact, I had stopped calling it a diary when I went off to college. Later, while achieving a certain amount of success in theater, I started wading knee-deep in Leonard's charm. There also was knee-deep bullshit, undermining a dangerously frail marriage. As I wrote about my husband in those days, the entries grew progressively angrier. The journal became a repository for painful feelings I dared express nowhere else.

It was not an uncommon practice of mine, after an argument with Leonard, to confess all in my journal. I often hid in my bedroom and typed like someone possessed. When I got that angst down on paper, I had such relief! It was just as if I blew every problem right out of the top of my head, like a volcano that spewed words instead of lava. Once those feelings were written down, I didn't always have to solve my marital problems in anger. The rage was carefully spelled out on paper, emotions hurled into the keys.

There were two possibilities. I could either throw aggravation out and forget what had happened, or hand a copy to Leonard to read in the quiet of the library. Let *him* fester! At least *my* feelings were spent.

It was this habit of setting down my vexations and disillusionments that saved me from having a breakdown after I had been married a few years. Writing meant more and more to me.

I believe that if I had let my frustrations out, vented my spleen verbally on Leonard (Collin got the fallout), I certainly would never have stuck with either Collin or Leonard. It was because I wrote about the problems of *staying* married, about returning to theater, that I was able to rise above the precipitous business of keeping my family intact and continuing to act at the same time.

If you read about movies and theater life, you will recognize the pitfalls. Such was my case. All the passion and jealousy and the tightrope balancing act of being a parent and an artist at the same time was a gigantic task. I don't feel I ever really was successful at it. If truth were known, simply staying attractive, fighting the battle of the bulge and facial stress lines all those years was hard enough, without marriage, childbirth, dealing with cloth diapers, school conferences, pediatricians, homework, discipline, and car pools.

As for writing itself, I had finally learned to use a typewriter by my college years. I typed my way through drafts of stories and papers, and after graduation, after the death of my formal education, came the death of the typewriter.

The world and I moved on to computers, so I transferred most of what I wanted to keep from the blue diary and the journals onto floppies. Sometimes, I think life has become as mechanical as learning to use a computer. It wasn't only writing modes that changed. I changed. Thoughts flew by; it was a faster world. It had been so much more satisfying mulling ideas over, then painstakingly setting down the words out through the fingertips into a pen and onto an empty page. From pens to tapped keys to electronic margins in less than one person's lifetime. Too fast and automatic. Too fast for someone who feels a kinship with Jane Austin. So strange to be reading back and forth between the blue-book pages and the computer pages on the desk in front of me. I can't help thinking life ends soon enough, without being reminded how fast my story flies.

When I met Collin, I was thirty-three, and that was the time when I began to change the most. There I was, transplanted from New York and our skyscraper apartment overlooking Seventy-ninth Street, moved by my tricky husband to the herbaceous hills of Connecticut. My journal is fat with entries about that time and about meeting Collin ... actually, about all of us.

So, I had become an actress for a few short years. Broadway, TV, the works. Then my creative life was over. The central essence of myself became dormant. Other than performing my duties as mother and wife, I saw no joyous reason to get up in the morning. I was in mourning. I also mourned the New York of the forties and fifties, of my teens and early twenties ...

It was simply a huge city, where sometimes part of the Essex House sign, to everyone's delight, read "sex House." Despite the sign, New York was a gentle city then. Everyone who lived there hung out in Central Park when they could, even in the evenings, walking freely without fear. Funny, I never thought of Central Park as the outdoors. It was surrounded by build-ings, after all. The word "mugging" didn't appear in the H*erald Tribune* or the *Times,* the two respectable newspapers. The biggest scandals told of embezzlements, while rapes were briefly alluded to in the *Daily News*. Rapes were too shocking to appear in most newspapers, unless they were a companion piece to murder.

Then the news became more brazen and violent. People started to protect themselves. Many experienced the crime secondhand by simply reading the newspapers. I was one such person; Collin, another. He read the *Daily News*.

Collin and I found that bad things could be contained, if we merely read about them. That was my mother's credo, too. It's a pity we couldn't have stayed that way. ⟞

 Entry Seven

⟞ One day, with my returned bank statement, I found a canceled check for $135 made out to some guy Collin knew. I kept the checkbook in my desk, as Collin was fully aware. Really upset, I asked if they were stealing from me. ⟞

COLLIN: (*earnestly*) Lady, the guy is in a drug rehab center. He was desperate when he found your checkbook.

BLAIR: (*enraged*) How did he find it? You must have shown him where I kept the checks. Why didn't you stop him? Tell me that. And don't call me Lady.

C O L L I N : He was snooping around. I didn't know till later. He must have searched your desk while I was working in the kitchen.

B L A I R : Are you stealing from me, Collin? If you are, I won't keep you here one minute longer.

C O L L I N : I would never do that to you. I swear. Let me pay it off . . . please.

B L A I R : (*disgusted*) You already owe me the last fare to France.

C O L L I N : Have a heart, Lady. I'll manage. I just feel sorry for the guy.

✍ I had to give him the benefit of the doubt or fire him. That was the first time theft had cropped up. Stealing is stealing. An accomplice is an accomplice. But then Collin reminded me that I had so much and this friend of his had so little, that I would reap the benefits in my next reincarnation.

Collin was into reincarnation big. He regularly went to the spiritualist church and received messages from Beyond. He had more friends who were dead than alive. He was as attracted to the mystical as I wanted to be. Years later, my daughter flew to California, joined a commune and became a spiritualist. Her explanations were more appealing to me than Collin's. He had hit me in the wrong way, but at the right time. As my parents aged, death was on my mind. Leonard said, "I'm not going to go to the police and have someone arrested for 135 bucks.

Besides, your son's friends aren't above stealing. You'd better keep your eye on them." *My* son, huh?

Leonard intercepted Collin in our library one day. He hadn't realized I was reading a scene for a local audition in the adjacent dining room and could hear every word they said.

LEONARD: Collin, I want to talk to you.

COLLIN: It's not about that stolen check again, is it? Because if it is, I'll just take off.

LEONARD: I don't want you to leave, Collin. The truth is, I like having you here with us. Blair and I don't fight as much with a third person present, and I like to know you're in the house with Blair, especially now that I'm planning to start a condominium project in Newport. I love my wife, Collin. Even if she thinks I don't. You're a companion to her, I can see that. It's good that she has someone around who's sensitive.

COLLIN: (*smiling*) I'm happy I can save the day, / helping her the way you say.

LEONARD: Beg your pardon?

COLLIN: Just one of my poems. I'm revising a few of them to submit to the *Lakeville Journal*. Maybe they could put one under the picture of the week. That paper sure could use a touch of artistry.

LEONARD: Well, that's fine, Collin. I won't admit this to Blair, but I miss doing creative work. Ahem, uh—like your rhyming.

COLLIN: I think you're creative. Remodeling houses is an art. And you were in the theater. The lady says you produced off-Broadway. That's talent, in my book. (*He and* Leonard *exit.*)

↩ Collin could be empathetic. He said he was an old soul. Leonard was pleased that Collin appreciated him. I didn't want to get rid of Collin, either. I felt comfortable with him from the very first ghastly rhymes that poured out of his mouth. We let the theft slide. ↩

Entry Eight

↩ Retribution was Collin's creed, although he would be horrified if you brought that up. Collin liked to talk about how religious he was. My foot! Collin's real agenda was to pay back anyone he thought had wronged him. That was *his* religion, although he saw many reasons to participate in the activities of the Episcopal church down the road from our house in Falls Village, when he wasn't called to the spiritualists.

Flipping back through my journal, I see that Collin went to church just about every Sunday he wasn't on a trip or at one of Leonard's properties. He knew the genealogy of everyone else who attended and had a nice social thing going, even before he came to work for us. Well, I thought he should indeed be speaking to God, if for no other reason than to ask forgiveness.

As much as he conversed, Collin had spells of being secretive, so you rarely knew what was bothering him. When I heard that silence like a bomb dropping, I knew my present grievance, like not letting him use my car on his day off, would cost me dearly. He would stalk out of the room, and that was the signal. I knew he would take the first opportunity he could find to reciprocate. One springtime incident was a good example. By then, due to a love of gardening Collin helped instill in me, I was spending quite a bit of time outdoors. ∽

BLAIR: What did you do with the clippers? I want to cut the lilac bushes back.

COLLIN: (*drying dishes*) It's too early in the season to cut them. I'll do it next week.

BLAIR: I want to do it now, Collin. Besides, I'd like to force a few. Cut them early and put them in water to blossom. You know our lilacs are my pride and joy.

(*silence*)

Collin, where are the clippers?

COLLIN: I like to do them. In order to get lilacs to bloom, / you shouldn't cut them off too soon.

BLAIR: You have a whole garden to worry about. Just give me the clippers.

COLLIN: They're lost. Mark must have borrowed them.

BLAIR: You know damn well Mark never gardened in his life. Now, where are they?

(*Silence.* Blair *looks under a pile of old towels in the laundry room and finds them.*)

(*angry*) You hid these, didn't you? Watch it, Collin, don't you lie, / or Blair Stewart will make you cry.

COLLIN: That's a lousy rhyme. You may have talent, but not for poetry. I'm not finishing these dishes! I feel sick now. You're always pushing me!

BLAIR: You know I have to go away next week. I need you to take over here, so Leonard and the children are fed and everything. We have a lot to accomplish,

COLLIN: I'm the one who needs a vacation. You make me crazy. There's nothing to live for. I'm so depressed I'm thinking of killing myself again. I'm going downstairs to the basement.

BLAIR: Collin, don't try that emotional blackmail. I'm counting on you. Just this morning you were outside weeding, whistling like a bird.

🖎 He gave me a black look and went off. I took the clippers and trimmed back the lilacs. I put a few in a vase and cleaned up the dinner dishes. He talked about killing himself when he was confronted and couldn't retreat into silence. Well, he hadn't! I made sure. I knocked on his door on my way to bed that night and he grunted and snarled, indicating I should get lost. I peeked in, and he was busy sorting through travel brochures.

When I came downstairs the next morning and immediately went outside, because I had a premonition, I saw what I should have expected. Collin had ruined my lilac plants. He had cut them so far back to the ground that they would never blossom that year. And, as if that wasn't bad enough, I found a note on the kitchen table. It said that he'd gone away for an indeterminate amount of time. He must have high-tailed it out at the crack of dawn. He said he was sorry if it inconvenienced me, compromised my own departure, but he simply needed to get away, right now, for his health. This was all about my challenging him. Now my own trip was out of the question.

Anything that Collin saw as a slight from anyone, he paid back with some vindictive act. You'd come home to find your new book missing or your favorite sweater shrunk. When you inquired, "How did this happen?," he knew nothing, saw nothing and turned his radio volume higher, smiling happily as Doris Day flew the ocean in a silver plane or Tony Bennett sang about the wonders of Chicago.

Once, we wouldn't let him use the car. He'd gotten two speeding tickets and didn't tell us. There followed what we called the "sour cheese incident." ↫

BLAIR: (*looking in refrigerator*) What's this rotten cheese doing in here?

COLLIN: What cheese? Where?

BLAIR: The refrigerator stinks! The milk's turned sour, too.

COLLIN: Smells fine to me.

BLAIR: It smells like hell, and you know it. Why'd you leave the cheese in there, Collin? You did it on purpose. And I know you *think* you have a reason.

COLLIN: You could have cleaned it out yourself, but you hate housework. Besides, that's your guilt talking. Guilt gives off a bad smell.

BLAIR: Guilt about what? What do you mean?

COLLIN: Not lending me the car to go into New York.

BLAIR: So you're paying me back?

COLLIN: (*amused*) Maybe God's paying you back. I'll pray for you in church. You need someone to pray for you. You missed taking Kay to her friend Nancy's for a sleep-over last week. You said you would, but you forgot. That's why *she's* not talking to you.

BLAIR: She's not talking to me? I didn't notice. Why didn't you take her?

COLLIN: I did. Her and Nancy. Then I drove them into town for chocolate-covered donuts. Nancy thanked me for always taking them wherever they wanted to go. I love the kids. I even took them to the movies. Nancy asked how come you had such a fancy kitchen and you barely ever cooked. I told her I had taken over that job, along with everything else.

BLAIR: (*wearily*) I used to love to cook, but it takes up so much time. I guess I'll have to apologize to Kay.

COLLIN: Don't worry about it, Lady. She understands. She also understands you hate cooking and dusting and keeping house, that you don't take up your time with these things. The kitchen is to me like the theater is to you. The spatula is a prop. I take the spatula and smooth my cakes so that the tops look store-bought. My corn rows in the garden are as straight as a ruled line. My carrots are a poem!

BLAIR: There's no question, you do have an artist's touch. The way you wax the tables so they look as smooth as glass.

COLLIN: I'm as proud of a well-kept home as you are of any character you create on stage. We both are artists, in our way. Nancy even admired the way each *tsatske* in the living room sits just so. She told me, "My mother is sloppy, just like Mrs. Stewart."

BLAIR: Thanks for the endorsement! And where'd you get *"tsatske"*? From my mother?

COLLIN: From you. You said it meant "trinket" in Yiddish. Someday I may travel to Israel.

BLAIR: Forget your trips. Are you telling me Kay and her friends say that I'm sloppy? That they discuss my personal habits?

COLLIN: (*calmly*) Now, don't get excited, Lady. Kay just said that's why you kept me. And if you let me have the car when I need it, the refrigerator will never have anything spoiled in it. I always keep my word, for a while.

BLAIR: That's sneaky, Collin! We have guests coming up from New York. I'll tell them the refrigerator is your responsibility.

COLLIN: Don't be so childish and self-centered. (*starts to leave*)

BLAIR: (*yells after him*) Take the car! Drive it! Get two more tickets. What do I care?

Entry Nine

⤳ Collin loved guests, but he hated them to see him "in waiting." He would help me prepare the house, the guests' rooms, the meals and then deliberately disappear, not to be seen or heard from again until the guests departed.

If he were to join us … that was very different. Collin was overjoyed when he was invited to sit down with our close friends for dinner, and that was often. Our lifestyle was casual; we didn't want to exclude him. One summer evening, Collin was at table with my cousin Joanie, and Bill Avery and John Johnson, two gay friends of ours, married to each other for all intents and purposes. Both decorators, they had lived together for twenty years. Bill had a sharp sense of humor. John, twelve years younger, was warm and enthusiastic, very family-oriented. They were used to Collin and found him amusing. ⤳

(Joanie, John, Bill, Leonard *and* Collin *enter and sit at the table.* Blair *joins them. Standing,* Blair *opens a box of fried chicken and puts pieces on plates.*)

JOANIE: Yum, yum, finger licking. Just what I don't need for my waistline.

BILL: In between husbands, I see. Do your dates complain?

JOANIE: Not if they want to live.

BILL: John ought to do something about *his* weight, don't you think?

JOHN: Remember what I told you about not sniping at me in public? I know about polite behavior, even though you've been on this earth two decades longer.

JOANIE: Oh, oh. Slings and arrows.

BILL: Sorry, John. You're perfect in every way, except you can't count. I'm only one decade older!

(Blair *sits. They all start to eat.* Blair *watches* Collin *chewing agonizingly slowly on a drumstick.*)

JOHN: Bill's niece just got married. We were at the wedding. You should have seen how beautiful she looked! A *princess.* I made her gown. Portuguese lace. The hem took me seven months. Sewed my fingers to the bone at night. Poor Bill was left to watch and weep.

JOANIE: (*sarcastically*) I didn't know you sewed, *too.*

BILL: I never weep. This man's talents never cease, Joanie. At least, that's what his date told me the other night.

BLAIR: *He* had a date, after all you mean to one another?

JOHN: (*feigned outrage*) What are you talking about, old man? That was no date. That was just a school friend who used to adore me in days of yore.

COLLIN: (*delighted*) That rhymes.

BILL: (*smiles*) Yeah, sure. Well, John, you're entitled. No one expects total loyalty.

LEONARD: Blair does. She's always jealous.

BLAIR: (*with admirable calm*) I can't help it. I have a flair for drama.

JOHN: No one ever *died* of jealousy. Least of all Bill.

BILL: Emotions wear daggers. People really do get sick from emotional turmoil and die.

JOHN: Not you, of course.

BILL: Never me, but watch it! One night I'll cudgel you in your sleep.

JOHN: No, you won't. You're too staid. (*to the others*) Oh, that wedding. I loved the whole day. Bill wore a new white linen suit I picked out. Bernice came down the aisle sooo radiant. They're going to Aruba on their honeymoon. I'm sending them a Steuben vase. Of course, they won't appreciate it. But they'll learn. You learn to love priceless things, when you get older.

BILL: Are you still talking about me?

JOHN: You're an illusion, Billy. It's some other poor idiot who's getting older. No, I just hope Bernice and her mate'll be as happy as we've been all these years. I may have talent, but Bill's introduced me to the world.

BILL: I protest. I've done nothing for the man. Just set him up in business, that's all. Maybe … done a little more. A bit of this and that.

JOHN: Bloomin' taught me everything I hadn't already picked up at Pratt Institute.

BILL: (*beaming*) Why be modest? I *did* teach him everything. He knew a good man when he met one. And look how suave he is. You think he was born that way? Look how fondly he looks at me. You'd think I was some young hunk, the way he carries on. Collin, why that expression on your face? What's the matter? You have something against our high-flying act, you little straight, you? Don't you *wish*?

COLLIN: Very funny.

JOANIE: Collin, why don't you get up and serve some soft drinks and stop looking so uncomfortable?

COLLIN: (*his mouth full*) MMMffflater.

JOANIE: (*whispers loudly in* Blair's *ear*) He's not going to do it. Why did I bother to ask? I know how perverse he is. You've been glaring darts at him for five minutes. Why don't you *make* him? *You're* his employer.

BLAIR: (*whispers back*) Nothing makes him budge if he doesn't want to! Look at him gnawing at that chicken. In another minute, he'll eat the bone.

JOANIE: I hope it sticks in his throat! (*changes subject*) God, John, I wish I could be as lucky as you. No one has excited me in a blue moon. I'm flying to Portugal next month, all alone.

BILL: (*to* Leonard) Talk about flying, what does your plane cost you? The way I figure, it would only take us five years of decorating triumphs to make up the down payment for one. Compared to you and Blair, we live scaled-down lives.

JOHN: Who needs money if you have charm? Are able to mooch? Blair, Leonard … say the word. We'll move in and put Collin out of a job. Blair, Darling, if this Kentucky Fried is any indication of how you saved up for Leonard's plane … forget it. Next time, I'm cooking Duck Mozambique. Can you do that, Collin? Ooops, I forgot. You're just a *guest* now. (*to* Bill) Skip the daydreams, Bill. We'll never buy airplanes. Besides, if you're rich, you have to play golf, and I loathe the game.

LEONARD: The plane hardly costs me anything. I have to go back and forth to Rhode Island, and it's a write-off.

JOANIE: (*persistent and pointedly*) Collin, Blair might like more chicken. Will you pass the serving tray? (*whispers to* Blair) Just watch! He's going to keep ignoring me. (*to* Collin, *sweetly*) Why don't you get the soft drinks, Collin? Pretend it's a play and you're the butler. Or whatever they call you. You're taking advantage. You know, you have no idea how democratic the Stewarts are, to let you join us for supper.

COLLIN: I'm not a butler. I just work here.

JOANIE: Then work.

COLLIN: Relax, Joanie. I'm listening to the men. Hold your horses. (*to* Leonard, *eagerly*) Tell them about the time you had engine failure and crash-landed at the Danbury Airport. Planes are so unreliable. I used to fly British Airways. They forgot to put the food on board for an international flight. That's why I prefer ships.

LEONARD: Collin, let's not get into ships, let's stick with planes. Well, you're really not supposed to talk about belly landings in flying circles.

BILL: Now it's flying circles, is it? Dear me.

JOHN: Dear, dear me.

LEONARD: There was nothing I could do. I was in the landing pattern, headed for the runway, and the landing gear malfunctioned. I tried it once, twice; nothing happened. My life with Blair passed before my eyes.

BLAIR: Sometimes you can be so sweet, Leonard. Collin, please clear the table.

JOHN: Was she flying, or doing a belly landing?

(*Everyone laughs.* Collin *remains seated.* Blair *gets up noisily. She snatches the paper plates and shoves them in the chicken box, staring at* Collin, *demanding he move. The guests at the table freeze and watch* Collin, *who is oblivious to them as he eats carefully, taking caution not to clack his false teeth while munching the salad. Angrily,* Blair *goes into the kitchen and soon returns with the dessert plates and dessert, juggling them precariously, then putting them on the buffet.* Collin *and* Leonard *ignore her. The boys snicker.* Blair *sits. The action at the table continues.*)

LEONARD: (*tearing a roll*) Nelson Graves told someone he's been running for office for ten years and has to pay a fortune to keep his face in the paper. "You turkey," he said. "You can't get your landing gear down and both your face and your plane hit the front page of the *News-Times* as big as life."

BILL: Does Nelson Graves need a decorator?

JOANIE: He's a politician, and he plays golf, John. Golfers and politicians don't decorate. Especially Nelson. The Graves mansion has had the same dismal furnishings for the last hundred years. I went to a New Year's Day party there. The upholstery was threadbare. So much for old money!

COLLIN: Is that the Graves who gave one hundred thousand to the Connecticut Symphony? Now that family comes from way back ...

BLAIR: No society tidbits, please. Nelson Graves is an idiot—against gun control and a woman's right to choose. Collin, could you please serve the dessert?

COLLIN: The pudding's closer to Bill.

JOHN: Bill doesn't do pudding.

(Bill *stares at* Collin, *then reaches over and puts the bowl on the table. When* Collin *doesn't lift a finger,* Bill *picks up the ladle and starts dishing out the pudding.*)

COLLIN: (*nicely*) That looks delicious. The lady can really make a good chocolate pudding. Bill, serve me a double portion.

JOANIE: (*whispers to* Blair) Fire him!

BLAIR: (*whispers back*) And who's going to clean up? You?

JOANIE: *Moi?* (*sweetly, to* Collin) Should you eat so much?

COLLIN: (*sincerely*) Oh, I never put on weight. It's the lady who has to worry.

(*The two cousins stare at* Collin, *fascinated that he is oblivious to the insult.* Joanie's *expression is murderous;* Blair *looks resigned. Only* Collin *is in motion, gobbling up the pudding.*)

JOANIE: (*pulls her cousin aside*) How can you let him get away with this?

BLAIR: (*whispering*) Did you ever look for domestic help? Yank that damned dish away from him before he licks off the glaze.

JOANIE: No way. (*hissing*) Mark my words, that guy has a primitive streak. You watch him And don't leave your jewelry lying about. He'll kill you for it, one day!

BLAIR: (*giggles*) Not for that. For squelching a trip to Europe, maybe. Jewelry … no. (*They return to table.*)

JOHN: Leonard, what happened next with the plane?

COLLIN: (*staring at* Leonard *in rapt attention*) Tell 'em, Leonard.

LEONARD: That's a good question. (*puffed up with pride*) Well, the fixed-base operator came looking for me, but I was long gone. He thought I must be on my way to the hospital. See, there were three guys waiting for me to play golf. Soooo … I just climbed out of the plane and made it to the club ten minutes before tee-off.

JOANIE: Is that supposed to be a joke?

JOHN: A golf joke, I suppose. What's fixed base? Sounds like a naval maneuver.

(Bill *gets up, pours the coffee and passes it around the table.*)

BLAIR: (*watching* Bill, *explodes*) Collin, Bill's pouring the coffee. You've been sitting during the whole meal, like royalty. Now do something!

COLLIN: (*half rises*) All right. Sorry. You invited me to eat with you. (*looks hurt*)

L E O N A R D : (*in mild reproach*) Blair, Sweetheart. Calm down! You really shouldn't yell at Collin like that, in front of guests.

(Collin *sinks slowly back onto his chair.*)

B L A I R : (*gritting teeth, snatching the coffee pot from* Bill *and pouring everyone's coffee but* Collin's) I can't do everything by myself. (*to* Collin) What's wrong with you, Collin? I'm not your mother, you know! (*to the others*) He's impossible!

J O H N : No, just a lousy butler. Collin, 'fess up. You know it's no reproach, coming from me. Aren't you gay?

C O L L I N : (*taken aback, annoyed*) Not on your life!

B I L L : Gauche, John. Really gauche.

J O H N : (*smiles innocently*) What's wrong? I just wanted to know. (*politely, to* Collin) I see. Bill was wrong. You're not gay. Two demerits for Bill.

B L A I R : (*trying not to laugh*) You're outrageous, John! Why are you so off the wall today?

L E O N A R D : Blair, everyone should say what they think. Isn't that fair? And stop talking about Collin as if he wasn't here. He's right in front of you.

C O L L I N : (*speaks good-naturedly*) I don't mind. The lady can't help it if she's a yeller. (*to all present*) She's an actress. (*warming to his subject*) Abdul O'Rourke directed her last month at the Mineola Playhouse showcase. There was a certain person in the cast she didn't like. You should have heard her yell. Then just last week ... I heard her rehearsing for an audition. A scene from *Macbeth*. A great Lady Macbeth. A natural, as we say in show business. Standing there wringing her hands, like she did when she looked at me just now. She even yelled at Macbeth when he didn't want to murder Duncan. But not as loud as she yells at me. (*He pours his own coffee.*)

BLAIR: (*furiously*) I don't need your reviews. I just want you to clear the table! Out, damned Collin!

LEONARD: You'd better watch her, Collin. Everybody, I advise you to remove all sharp objects. (*Amused,* Leonard *clears the wine glasses. He picks up the half-empty coffee pot and starts to take it out.*)

BLAIR: Leonard, please stop that! You're the host. Let Collin do it.

LEONARD: What the hell. I don't mind. Let Collin finish his pudding. (Leonard *starts out with the coffee pot.*)

COLLIN: Hold on, Leonard. Pour me a little more, will you? Coffee's the best part of the meal. (*All watch as* Leonard *carefully, patiently, pours the rest of the coffee into* Collin's *cup.*)

BILL: The story, for God's sake, Leonard. You left the plane on the runway. How did the golf game go?

LEONARD: I beat the pants off Nelson. Got an eagle on the third. And he thought he had tied it with his birdie.

JOHN: What's a birdie? Why not a doggie or a hoggie or a bunny or a titmouse, for that matter? Tied it with a titmouse. Bravo!

BILL: Never mind that. What's an *eagle?*

J O H N : These men are grown-ups? *Birdies?* Sounds like a fairy tale to me.

B I L L : Right up your line. Maybe they'd like you to take them cruising.

(*They freeze as* Collin *contentedly sips and* Leonard *laughs and exits, balancing the rest of the coffee cups on a tray.*)

꙼ After the chicken scene ... well, I could understand Collin's mother ... I wouldn't have minded tying Collin to a tree and beating the shit out of him. Still, we went on living together and refurbished houses together, with decorating help from John and Bill. Collin did for us what he had done for Mrs. Marlin: wallpapered and painted bedrooms, moved furniture and packed boxes. The truth is, he was invaluable.

Collin loved working in the garden as much as ever. He was painstaking, but a sloppy weeder. He was generally meticulous in everything else he did. He was wonderful at a lot of things. Refinishing furniture, and cooking. Cooking slowly, but so what? And he loved our dogs, cared for them with a passion some men reserve for mistresses.

I was hooked on Collin, I guess. With children, a part-time husband, two elderly parents out of town, a house always being remodeled, dogs, and a crazy career—ask any woman who's been there. Did I have a choice? The house was filled with guests, mostly the children's friends, and our vegetable and flower gardens seemed to get bigger each year. Collin could have done almost anything and I wouldn't have dared fire him. ꙼

Entry Ten

⌒ Despite myself, I became enthralled with the beautiful Connecticut countryside. My walks with the dogs, with Collin, with the children, or even alone, became a magical experience. My body felt toned because I was walking an hour or more each day. I would leave the house early, before the morning mist disappeared. Nearby, there was a field studded with boulders. Birds of stunning color dove from oak to hemlock to maple, and wildflowers of all shapes and hues poked their heads through the meadow grasses.

Every so often I'd pass a neighbor selling old books and fascinating bric-a-brac, some handcrafted and some dime-store junk, in his barn. He and his wrinkled, smiling wife let me prowl to my heart's content. Sometimes I'd pick up another *tsatske* for Collin to place and dust.

Early in the day, the light in the sky made me feel overwhelmingly happy. More and more, I forgot New York, with its hot sidewalks and sparse, soot-layered trees.

Life was good. I had more energy than ever before. A

general aura of well-being overtook me. Happiness was descending. As Collin concentrated on the garden, I gradually resumed cooking and created imaginative, nourishing meals. Kay and Mark, turning eleven and twelve that summer, were flying through the house in their bathing suits as they headed to the pool, which Leonard had installed in the spring, or out to the fields to run and whisper with their friends and admire the glorious weather that had sparked all our enthusiasm.

Leonard and I were becoming more experimental in bed. First, he started one innovation; then it would be my turn. We laughed a lot together, and our sex life was exciting. I worried less about the long-haired nymph flirts, who seemed to be aging before my very eyes. Several of them had gone to college and come home with live-in boyfriends or looking shopworn. They weren't such hot competition anymore. I felt newly sure of myself, sensuous and secure. I had decided that I would share some of this new womanliness with my husband, but keep a hidden reservoir for as yet undetermined activities.

In the height of the summertime, Collin's father died at the Torrington nursing home. Collin didn't find out for two days, until he called the home to ask for a report on his father's condition. ⮌

COLLIN: (*enraged*) They never even told me. *Nobody told me!* The home called Mom's place and talked to my brother.

BLAIR: Oh, I'm so sorry. Sorry you lost your father. It wasn't entirely unexpected, was it?

COLLIN: (*jaw set*) I didn't like him much. He was never really nice to us. But he was my father, and my brother should've told me. It was just spite that he didn't. Or he wanted to get the few bucks Dad had left, before I found out.

BLAIR: Any money should go to your mother. She's his widow. What are you going to do? Are you going to the funeral?

(Collin *mutters something and slams the door.*)

✐ I called the Episcopal church to ask about the Williams' services. The funeral was set for the next afternoon in Falls Village. Collin scarcely spoke all that morning. Kay and Mark, dressed in pale summer cottons, accompanied me to the cemetery. We stood graveside watching them lower the coffin into the ground. We were standing in back, away from the small nucleus of the family: Collin's brother, who exuded alcohol; his sister; his mother, looking dazed and soft in shirtwaist and skirt; and several friends and neighbors, including Hezzy in a starched white shirt and too-hot flannels. ✐

KAY: (*whispers*) Mom, why's Collin acting so strange? He nearly knocked the minister over when he poured the wine. Collin was twitching. Then, he dropped the wafers off the tray.

MARK: Look at him! He hasn't even bothered to change from his jeans and sneakers. What's the matter, didn't he like his father?

BLAIR: (*whispering*) He's furious with his whole family.

He's been slamming doors all morning.

KAY: I didn't even know Collin's father, but I'm wearing dressy shoes. It's only polite.

BLAIR: Don't criticize poor Collin. He drives you to school, fixes you goodies to eat.

KAY: (*hissing quietly*) He tattles on me all the time.

MARK: (*snickers*) He does worse than that.

BLAIR: What do you mean?

MARK: Never mind. Shhh!

MINISTER: (*about to lower the coffin into the earth*) Would anyone like to say some words of remembrance, before we send Mr. Williams to his rest?

(*Silence.* Collin *stares meanly at his sister and brother and breaks wind deliberately and loudly.* Mark *cracks up laughing behind his hand. The minister's face reddens as he gives the signal to lower the coffin.* Collin's *sister stamps her foot and leaves.* Collin's *mother, practiced at overlooking her children's actions, stares straight ahead. The brother bumps into a tombstone and belches.*)

KAY: (*to Blair*) Gross! I'm so embarrassed, I could die. He made a tushy burp on purpose.

MARK: (*splitting his sides laughing*) I think it was great! Way out! (*puts his mouth against the back of his hand and starts making gaseous noises*) Boy, that was some fart. Wait'll the guys hear about this.

BLAIR: (*teeth clenched*) Just watch your language. Remember where you are! We call that breaking wind. Don't let the behavior of others influence *you.* As for Collin, I'm going to have a talk with him when we get home.

(Blair *drags her son and daughter across the lawn. Standing aloof* Collin *glares at his remaining family, a savage look on his face.*)

↫ Collin stormed around all week, and I never did get a chance to talk to him. He created bedlam in the kitchen by knocking together the pots and pans. He drowned the pansies in the window box and shrank my black wool sweater in the dryer. My strategy, learned from him, was silence. I just ignored him.

Finally, he had enough. Collin placated us by roasting a fabulous stuffed chicken on Sunday. He was some cook, when he wanted to be. I had to thank him after we ate. He knew I would. He knew that amnesty was one key to keeping his job.

I broke the silence, and the week of anger dissipated. It mingled with the fragrance of the juicy bird and fresh vegetables he had retrieved from the garden that morning. The aroma that filled the kitchen was like a gentle benediction.

If retribution was Collin's faith, the secret of compromise was his art. All I could think about, at that time, was thanking God I was acting again. Yes, I had put my newfound energies into a string of auditions.

How soon we forget our prior troubles. I won roles in various Connecticut theaters, becoming more and more absorbed, forgetting about making new friends and shopping and home life and loneliness. I stopped cooking. Leonard was happy marketing his condos. What did it matter that he seemed a little distracted? I thought I would make it up to him as soon as one play was over, and then the next. But the next was too good not to follow up with one more challenging role. Collin picked up the out-of-town newspapers and started clipping my reviews, good, bad or mixed.

When I wasn't rehearsing or memorizing lines, Collin offered temptation with the chivalry of bygone days. He had learned the secret of how to keep me loyal forever. It was chocolate and nuts. As simple as that. We both were chocolate freaks, both candy hiders, closet sweet eaters if criticized. He knew the good chocolates from the cheap stuff, as I did. He knew I was so bad, I'd hide the Toblerones from the kids and give them supermarket candy bars. So he got smart. Collin learned how to create the perfect brownie.

He had, on the sly, swiped from the *New York Times Cook Book* a fabulous recipe. Not just for cake brownies—but gooey, chewy, nutty ones. Collin's brownies blew me away. This won Collin many, *many* more days of employment and much praise and periodic forgiveness, as the need arose. The days spun by, habit took over, and it seemed Collin would be with us forever.

Leonard told me how happy he was with Collin's cooking and how well the house looked. Leonard was spending a good deal of time away these days. Was I jealous? Of course not. An actress feels no jealousy, except toward another actress who tries to upstage her. Leonard was right. For me, people outside the play simply didn't exist.

Leonard was still convinced I needed Collin, and I was convinced Leonard needed him. Leonard couldn't fix anything, and Collin fixed everything. And Leonard, of course, was still disappearing, leaving Collin my sole adult companion.

Collin knew where we kept the plans for the house and when we repaired what, much better than I did. He knew where we kept the mortgage papers and when we had invested in a new roof and when our friends' birthdays were and when our children's vacations were scheduled. Who else knew those things? He was a walking chronicler. And does the queen banish the court scribe? Never. The queen is grateful someone thinks enough of her life to keep track of it. ⤙

 Entry Eleven

⤙ My former agent called out of the blue. She wanted to know if I would audition for a soap opera on ABC. My ego screamed, "No!," but my voice paid little attention. I eagerly replied, "When and where?"

In the morning Collin arose at five to drive me to the Stamford railroad station, the best commute with the most trains. Selecting and discarding clothes and putting on the right makeup, I had been up since four. Leonard had spent the night in the guest room to get out of the way. Because we beat the rush hour down into Fairfield County, Collin and I had time to breakfast in Westport at the diner where Paul Newman sometimes hung out. He wasn't there.

The grubbiness and disrepair of the train to New York had not changed. As I sat in a grimy coach, I thought of many things—of Thanksgiving just passed, with all the pleasant preparations: shining silver with Kay; Collin arranging dried flowers he'd picked in the woods, as well as acorns and gourds, for the centerpiece; and the safe, happy sensation of Leonard nearby, watching the ball game with Mark on our enclosed porch. Thanksgiving had been my day and my show. No try-outs necessary.

Today I was cold with nervousness. The old, familiar lump was there in my stomach. It always preceded auditions in New York. If you can make it there, you can make it anywhere, the song challenged. It had been years since I'd "made it." They had-n't told me then that you have to *keep* making it. Once is never enough. I looked at my reflection in the train's streaked windows and cursed my sparse dark hair, which only looked right in neat, groomed waves. My mature features would not support a breeze-swept style. Television actresses should have thick, tumbling hair to go with those sleek bodies. My body had thin limbs and a womanly torso. I saw the passing of the years on my face, a mesh of tiny lines around the eyes and mouth.

In this business, confidence is everything. Mine was wavering. I thought of my women friends who remained in show business, year after year. They sold themselves daily to producers and casting agents, rarely getting the part they wanted. But hope was an eternal flame. Around the next corner waited success. In my mind, I heard their conversation.

"Are you working?"

"Yes. "

"In a show?"

"Not right now, but I had an audition today."

The train grumbled and reluctantly moved on. Soon, here was the Harlem stop, then the complex of tunnels and the lower level of Grand Central. I strode upstairs and found a cab. I had to pick up the script at Keel and Simon Casting, where my former agent, Marissa Keel, was waiting for me.

She had amazingly large breasts and bottom and the faint remainder of a southern accent she tried to conceal. Marissa had always been a closet bulimic. She never stopped eating and kept disappearing into the john to throw up her latest snack. We chatted often in the days when I used to drop by to dig out the casting dirt. I was jubilant then and spoke to myself in confident tones. On this occasion, my internal dialogue raged.

"Take a close look at me, Marissa. I haven't changed much, have I? Perhaps I'm not right for ingenues anymore, but certainly mature roles … ? Am I still pretty? What do you think, do I fit into your acting stable? I'm back on the market— maybe not exactly kicking, but still alive."

I would slit my throat before I uttered one such thought.

Inside the agent's office I took the script from the secretary, resisting an impulse to drop into Marissa's lair, like old times. On my way to Joanie's apartment (she had left me a key), I sat in the cab and opened the sides, the two complete scenes I was to read later at the network. I began to read. Soon, I was muttering Charlotte's incredible lines, the likes of which I could be saying for the next two years. This was a sample: ✑

CHARLOTTE: You've wined me, my darling Ray, and shared this sumptuous meal with me. We have dined on pheasant and champagne, and you have never once mentioned what this reunion is all about. Is it a new beginning, my darling? Are we to celebrate and toast the rebirth of our love? (*looks deep into his eyes, raises wine glass in a graceful toast*)

RAY: No, this is *not* a beginning, it is the end, my darling. (*with an effort toward lightness*) I want a divorce. (*stonily*) This time I mean it.

CHARLOTTE: (*in a voice like ice*) For that you must wait till the end of time.

End of scene.

✑ I was stunned. Leaving the cab, entering Joanie's building and empty apartment, I settled down and prepared to try to personalize the woman who could be saying those words. It wasn't going to be easy.

The more I read the lines, the more I thought this was not the reaction I would have to a husband who wanted a divorce.

I'd probably say, as Leonard was backing out the door, something like, "You must be crazy!" or "Over my dead body!" or, even more likely, "Get lost, you shit! I don't care what you do anymore. I haven't cared for years. Good riddance! Go mess up somebody else's life."

I was warming to this creative process.

Aloud, I said, "Thank God! I thought you'd never leave." Sounded on target.

I'd better stick to the script, I decided. If that's what turned a television audience on, I'd give it a try. I took a seltzer from Joanie's refrigerator and returned to the couch to ponder the second scene.

My character spoke to somebody named Meryl. ⌒

CHARLOTTE: The fact that I slept with your father, Meryl, before we lived together, should make you realize all the more this was a love match greater than the one with Harry, and always has been. No matter what Enrique told you. I loved your father deeply, Meryl, even more than Reginald or Jeffrey. (*voice catches*)

We have been together, Ray and I, for a long time, as you have just reminded me in such an accusatory fashion. Yet I have been miserable, my dearest one, miserable. Have you any idea what it cost me, living with his selfishness? With his outbursts? Don't you think I know about all the women he has had? About Agatha, Françoise, Maria and Gretchen? About Ming Toy and Towanda?

⌇ Good grief, I thought. This guy's worse than Leonard. ⌇

MERYL: (*weeping*) Oh, Mother, I don't know what to believe. Enrique says all sorts of gossipy things. He's getting as bad as Lionel, the time he caused such trouble between me and Cynthia.

CHARLOTTE: My heart goes out to you. I do understand! I remember. It was always like that. Crying doesn't help, poor child. I ought to know. (*takes Meryl in her arms*) Now dry your tears, my sweet. I know you don't mean to hurt me. Your father is taking me out to dinner tonight. Perhaps we can talk it out. There'll be two of us to convince him. Two of us, Meryl, together. You and me. I pray he loves us enough.

⌇ Then there was a note written by the director: "to be followed by kiss-off." Too bad it was penciled in; it was the best line in the script. I read both scenes over and over, until I understood the character. A pity she wasn't more real. Her speeches were so overblown, they were practically unlearnable.

I changed into a taupe suit I'd brought with me. The suit was right for the part, but it was silk, and I would probably freeze on this cold December day. Going for a part always put adrenaline in my blood; that would warm me up. Next, I put my running sneakers, socks and a heavy woolen pullover into a shopping bag, along with the script and my picture with the résumé on the back, and took a taxi down to the studio, teeth chattering. I felt as if the people on the street were characters out of some larger soap opera. I started to tremble, but wouldn't permit it. I would be playing the role of a mature, confident woman, a woman I was no longer. I watched the dark-dressed city people on the sidewalks. Navy, brown, especially the usual black. Few children—too cold, I supposed. Soon I was there.

"Is this ABC?" I asked a tall actor leaving the building. It was just a stall. Obviously this was the place, judging from a coven of other actors standing around, probably exchanging casting tips.

"Four flights up." He smiled, showing off his obnoxiously even white teeth. Caps, no doubt. Another of the perfect people you see in ads. I considered leaving then and there, except behind me stood a studio technician waiting for me to get into the elevator. I had no option but to ascend.

Behind glass doors a security guard pushed a button, so I could enter. He asked my name and, with a solemn expression, ticked it off on a sheet of paper on his desk. I smiled politely, as he returned to his seat and picked up the phone. His nod appeared to be dipped in disdain for our breed. I inched through the door and walked toward a group of women on a sofa and surrounding folding chairs. On legs that felt mummified, I joined them. Some were glancing through scripts; others pretended indifference.

No two looked at all alike, even though they were trying out for the same part, I surmised. A few looked as if they should be reading for *Anna Christie* rather than Charlotte. There was tension in the room, the chill of competitiveness. A few contenders were freshly coiffed, not long descended from hair dryers. Some had dyed hair and their roots showed it. Out of the corner of my eye I saw a possible "Mrs. Right." This woman seemed what they were looking for—a rejected upper-class New York matron. She wore little makeup and, wouldn't you know it? Her hair was thick and naturally sand-blond. She appeared haughty and unconcerned. Upon closer inspection, they *all* started to look right for the role.

You are neurotic and weak, I told myself, deciding to concentrate on the women more likely wrong for the part. My spirits had nowhere to go but up.

Two others had healthy, thick manes of hair. One was dressed in leather pants, à la Hollywood; the other wore a checkered, woolen poncho, like an aging Greenwich Village hippie. She was wasting her time here, I was glad to observe. They would never pick her! The one in the pants was TV thin. She had no bosom, but those pants choking her thighs were an asset, if she would be reading for a male producer. She announced she was here on a call back and had to postpone her return flight west. Of course, that was to tell the whole group that she was a strong choice. And she also meant it was no real concern of hers whether she got the part, because she had bigger fish to fry back on the West Coast, read California, read Hollywood.

A call back gave her an edge. She cowed everyone else. The

rest of us squirmed in our seats. Tight Pants was obviously a working actress in demand. Her signal threw the rest of us into visible rivalry. We went back to our scripts. I tucked my own listless strands of hair behind my ears. I fingered my pearls. I acted the lady, still and calm. There was a smooth coolness between my fingers. The pearls—I had put on real ones by mistake. What had I done? Where were my twenty-dollar fakes? If you don't look as if you need work, you won't get it. I wedged the pearls down under my collar, behind the silk bow.

We waited and waited. A swan-necked woman asked me, "Do you cast shows? You look familiar."

She probably had a dim recollection of our off-Broadway theater. I had sent out the casting calls. Len had handled auditions; he would never have chosen her. Too predictable-looking.

I smiled and shook my head.

Swan Neck appeared disappointed. A possible door to future work was closed, so she didn't even glance at me again. I was just another actress to compete against.

A woman with baubles swinging on her wrists skipped out of the corridor, script in hand, having just auditioned. She was a bit overweight, yet sure of herself. She spoke to Tight Pants of California.

"Good to see you, Sheila. Sorry you moved to the coast. Used to see you more often."

"I'm back and forth. Covering all fronts. What about dinner? Looks like I'm stuck here another day."

The plump one had flaming red curls, like a nine-dollar Little Orphan Annie wig. She was dressed, inappropriately, in jeans. I disliked her for her puppy-dog cuteness and confidence and her friendships with women who were making it in New York.

"Can't do dinner," she told Sheila. "Not tonight. I'll call you."

"We'll call *you*," I answered silently.

"What am I doing here, auditioning for television?" I asked myself. "I don't even *watch* television."

My alter ego whispered, "For the warmth of the lights, the attention, the excitement, the chance to be recognized." I had starred on television at twenty-one. Surely I knew more now than I had then.

I watched the redhead leave, swinging her bag, waving jauntily at Sheila and the others. This city was a playpen for an old hand such as she. I would have been the same way, if I hadn't left and gone with Leonard ... or had the children ... or gotten married in the first place. In fact, I would be a lot farther along than she. Self-confidence must be contagious.

Abruptly I was called, ushered into the corridor, and then into the room where I was to read. At the table, alone, sat Fay Taylor. I was surprised she was no longer working for CBS. I knew her pretty well in those days. Even her new casting office looked like the one at CBS, because she had hauled that huge avocado plant with her, and it had grown so big, it was choking out light from the smallish room, which faced an alley. I wondered why all casting offices faced alleys and had a glaring overhead fluorescent light that made it so hard to read the script. I guessed someone up there didn't care much for casting people. Or actors. Of course, this was a preliminary reading. The final dozen or so contenders would read in a studio before the director and his entourage.

I handed her my résumé, even though she must have had copies on file. She nodded to the chair opposite her. ⌐

FAY: Hello, Blair. Your name came up. That's why I had my secretary call your agent. What have you been doing for the last few years?

BLAIR: Writing. (*glibly*) As well as a few showcases and cameos, up in Connecticut and Long Island.

FAY: (*bored*) Sounds interesting. Have you read the script?

BLAIR: Glanced at it.

FAY: Is there anything you need to know about this part?

BLAIR: I want to know if my character is hurting. Is she devastated by her husband's affairs, by his leaving her, or pretending grief and happy to have him gone?

RAY: (*automatically*) All of it.

BLAIR: (*confused*) Does she think Meryl is a brat, or has she real compassion for her innocence?

FAY: (*picking at a cuticle as though her fingernail were an emerald*) It doesn't make much difference.

BLAIR: (*more agitated*) Then what *should I* know about my character?

FAY: (*The cuticle enchants her. Her attention is riveted on her finger.*) The husband and the wife have something on each other. They have to be cautious, act carefully, as each can blackmail the other. But, of course, you've seen the show.

BLAIR: (*lying*) Not lately.

✍ I meant, *not ever!* Mentally I sorted out how to act guarded, fearful of blackmail, devastated, full of pretense and, incidentally, happy at the same time. I wondered why Fay was staring at me. Was she wondering if I had the guts to carry this role each day? Was she wondering if my stage presence would still adapt to television?

"We should start," she said.

I put my hand inside my big pouch bag, but the script was not there. It had to be there, I just had the damned thing. Frantically I looked through the bag among the sneakers and other belongings. The script had vanished. "I had it in the waiting room," I said.

My panic seemed to confirm Fay's worst suspicions. I must have seemed, if too citified for country life, too countrified on this occasion for the big city. You could take me out of Falls Village, but you couldn't take Falls Village out of me. There I was, more flustered than when I had read for my roles during college.

"Never mind. Here's another one." Fay handed it over.

I flipped some pages. There was a buzzing, a high whine, as if someone were drilling concrete in the next room. Fay didn't seem to notice. I realized the words on the script suddenly possessed the ability to jump off the page. They hurled into space and bounced back in my eyes—little arrows that blurred my sight. I couldn't manage to pin the sentences down. They seemed to ricochet past my understanding. I felt I was levitating; reality disappeared.

I must know how to save myself, I had been an actress for years. Stop for a moment. Be silent, be clever. Remain suspended ... work with that levitated feeling ... above the panic. Somehow I must fill the void with my own canny power to endure. I was past the point of wanting the part; I was ready to settle for saving face. Besides, in no way could I make Fay believe that I believed in this script. It was too phony. In a burst of comprehension, I realized I had broken faith with make-believe. This wasn't fun any longer.

I felt supremely sad. All those years spent honing my craft, doing Shakespeare, Shaw, Molière, Tennessee Williams—to recite this trash? This mindlessness, projected into millions of homes between a housewife's lunch and ironing? Imagine saying lines like that for the next two years.

Pride dictated that I try. I read to Fay. The speeches echoed back, false and fake. I glued my eyes to hers (eye contact is vital), trying to appear intense and convincing. Fay's focus looked hazy, her eyes filmed over. Could she be weeping? Was I that good? Or were her thoughts elsewhere? I hammered home the "end of time" line. It was hard not to notice Fay's distant expression. She was probably wondering if her roast had thawed, or whether she and her actor-husband would go out to dinner. Who would pay? *She* would pay. *Her* job was steady.

Personally, I never believed those soap opera characters; but people told me thousands of viewers hung on every line and episode, to the point where they mailed wedding gifts and baby presents to the network.

Weakly I smiled at Fay. She said my reading was great, in a kind voice, which translated into, "You didn't get the part."

Relief was my reaction as I left. In the ladies' room I put on socks, sneakers and a sweater over my silk jacket. My suede heels went into the bag.

Through New York City I ran, in love with the smells, even the ones from garbage pails, and the screeching sounds of traffic. Just looking at the cracks in the sidewalk made me jubilant. I darted through streets more dangerous than when I'd lived in the city. Heading east, I slowed, panting, and power-walked toward Grand Central. My stamina was not what it used to be. I passed groups of men with sullen faces in ominous, silent conclaves, nary a policeman in sight. Down the street, a man sold watches from a table with tripod legs that could fold, if he had to move on. Elegant women entered hotel lobbies through polished brass-trimmed doors opened by liveried doormen. Men in navy or gray suits, holding newspapers under their arms, waited for business contacts or lovers. At a few large parties, I'd received invitations to meet someone's husband in the city "for lunch." The conversation usually began, after a one-on-one exchange of mild flirtation, "Do you get into the city often?"

These men were invariably commuters, invariably married,

and invariably looking for something beyond a lunch date. When I had been angry with Len, I sometimes had been tempted. But I hadn't been really interested in following through—although, I admit, it was good to be asked.

I wasn't scared, walking alone in New York. Give me all this any day. The city streets felt safer than waiting in that den of competing actresses, who couldn't wait to read such a script aloud and believe in it.

Inside the railroad station, I walked down the marble stairs and saw that an express to Stamford, stopping only at 125th Street, was leaving in twenty minutes. I had plenty of time to call Collin, who would meet me at the Roger Smith Hotel, where I would have a belated lunch. I was ravenous. The lump in my stomach had gone.

The Stamford Barn Theater had scheduled auditions for *Glass Menagerie* the following week, for a performance in February. I'd be fabulous as Amanda. At least, I could stand to say her lines. I'd practice a southern accent on Collin. He'd tell me I was great. What's more, he'd mean it. ⤸

Entry Twelve

⤸ Another point in Collin's favor was that I could talk intimately with him about my girlfriends' marital problems and about their children, which one had a drug addiction, who dropped out of school or won a scholarship, who got pregnant and who got an impressive job. Collin enjoyed dissecting all that. So did I. He was good company. Although Leonard was right: Collin became quite the spy. He overheard everything that Leonard said or whispered on the phone or behind closed doors or anywhere else, for that matter. The house was wall-less. Collin remembered it all! He understood immediately, when he eavesdropped on Leonard, what a word here or a phrase there might signify. And the best and worst of it was, when I asked what Leonard had been up to, God help me, Collin *told* me.

There was the time I had auditioned for a play in Westchester County, New York. Collin had just made the family a whole bunch of brownies, the day I found out I got the part. ⌐

BLAIR: Children, Leonard, I have great news! Tony called. He's casting me in Agatha Christie's *Mousetrap*. I'm so thrilled he picked me.

LEONARD: Congratulations, Honey. I'm happy for you. When will you start rehearsing?

MARK: Good for you, Mom. (*anxiously*) You're sticking around, aren't you, Dad?

LEONARD: Probably. Anyway, Collin will be here.

COLLIN: Congratulations. I love that play.

KAY: It's a stupid play. Are you sure you want to do it, Mom? What about my slumber party?

BLAIR: It's only three weeks' rehearsal, two weeks' playing. Time'll go by fast, Kay, Love. We'll plan your party anyway.

↬ The children talked some more about the play while we gobbled up Collin's brownies. We told him we were enthralled with his culinary talent. Don't say the heart isn't swayed by the taste buds, as well as other glandular secretions.

In a few days, I went off to rehearsals in Tarrytown and left Collin home to feed my kids. Kay's party was to be the following week. Mark, who had turned seventeen that fall, could think of nothing but track. I, at forty-two, was just happy to have them all out of my hair. Leonard was forty-five last summer. I barely noticed his comings and goings while I isolated myself at home, learning my part.

This was to be my first professional stage appearance in two years, not just a showcase, like *Macbeth* at the Sharon Playhouse or *Menagerie* in Stamford. This was to take place in a stock company near New York City. I would be paid Equity scale, and I would be reviewed, with luck, in the New York papers.

I was very nervous all week as we rehearsed at the Tarrytown Playhouse. I was playing Miss Casewell, the sister of the murderer. She was a masculine type, an aggressive lady with witty observations and sarcastic lines. This required walking and sitting with movements and mannerisms not my own. It meant I had to lower my voice and practice barking out my speeches.

The days fled by; the rehearsals were a challenge. I came home each night to sweet inquiries from my family as to how things were going. Suddenly, I found myself living the life I had always desired. What more could I want? I had paid my dues in life, had a husband and children and was now back to the career I loved so dearly. What could ever go wrong again?

Never be smug. Something always comes up to trip you. Maybe Satan put a wire across my path.

Dress rehearsal was soon upon us. Before I left the house, I received a call from my cousin. She was in Connecticut, having sublet her co-op for a fortune to an Arab diplomat. ⌒

(Blair's *phone rings*. Joanie *enters, holding a receiver to her lips.*)

BLAIR: Hi, it's you. Can't talk now. I have to rehearse. I'm so excited. Things are going so well. Leonard took off to play golf in the Keys, and I have the whole weekend to study my part.

JOANIE: You know I've been working at Leonard's office this week. I hate to burst your bubble, but I don't think he's alone. I overheard something.

BLAIR: (*anxiety written over her face*) God, what?

JOANIE: I think he was talking to that idiot actress he had the hots for during your show last summer. I think I recognized her voice. I heard him telling her, "You can get a bathing suit down there." He was speaking real low, and then he made a call to the travel agent.

BLAIR: I can't stand this. What did he say?

JOANIE: He was making changes. Charging one ticket to his account and a second to the business. I only heard a little, but he didn't have *me* put through the calls. I didn't think it felt right.

BLAIR: I think it stinks, that's what! (*Hangs up and slumps. Blair's face is between her hands, script before her. Collin enters. He and Blair sit at the table.*)

COLLIN: What's wrong? Worried about your opening?

BLAIR: It's not my opening. It's what Joanie heard. Do you think Leonard has someone with him in the Keys? Tell me straight, Collin. I want to know.

COLLIN: (*with glee, relieved to be asked*) I'm sure it's that fat-assed actress friend of his—that Laurie, all right. She called him last week and I heard a kind of simpering laugh. I'm sure it was that bitch, the one you let stay with us up here when you did the Shaw play. And she wouldn't wash her own sheets and towels so Leonard made *me* do it. When I complained, *he* washed them. You were wild! I heard them on the phone together. They didn't talk exact dates, but Leonard said he wanted to go down there. He was panting on the phone, so it had to be her. He practically slobbered while she was at the house.

BLAIR: Oh God, Collin. Are you sure? (*He nods.*) What am I going to do? I'm shaking all over. (*stands up and paces back and forth*) Why does he pick such pigs? Other actors clean up after themselves. She treated *me* like a servant, too. She's probably in my house in Florida right now, rolling around on my sheets and leaving them dirty on the floor again. In *my bed* with *my husband* who's not so neat either. Oh, I hate laundry!!!

COLLIN: (*uncertainly*) You don't look in any shape to drive to Tarrytown. I'll take you.

⇐ So Collin drove me to the theater while I ranted and raved, in my newly established dyke voice, about how I was going to kill Leonard and then, in the next moment, I was wild because I thought I was losing him. Thank heaven I knew my lines, because I was in no condition to *think*. The dressing room in Tarrytown was cold and gloomy. ⇐

(Blair *sits at dressing room table, facing out. She straightens her makeup and starts to apply it fitfully.* Collin *sits right behind her, enthralled.*)

COLLIN: You do that so well.

BLAIR: I'm good at makeup. (*remembers her part and lowers her voice*) I'm good at makeup. But I feel terrible. (*speculating, studying her face, applies lip liner and speaks in a natural voice*) How do I sound?

COLLIN: Like a lady truck driver. That liner really fills out your lips. Would Miss Casewell have full lips?

BLAIR: What do you want, a mustache? I need some glamour tonight. Hand me the eye pencil. The dark brown one.

(*drawing in thick brows*) I'll have it rough. A woman alone with two dogs and two children will be alone forever. I'll never find another man.

COLLIN: Some men like dogs. Besides, you're pretty and talented. Don't worry, I'll stay with you after the divorce. You'll be all right. (*putting a dab of color on his own brows*) Brown's not really my color.

BLAIR: Give me that! What divorce? Why bother? How could I ever trust anyone again?

COLLIN: You'll find someone. Meanwhile … we'll get along.

BLAIR: (*in a deep voice*) Maybe I should turn lesbian.

COLLIN: (*heartfelt*) Don't. You won't like it.

BLAIR: How have I been so naive? I knew what theater was like. Even if Leonard's no longer an actor, he was one. Actors have affairs. But I thought *we* would be different. We were so in love. We walked hand in hand, decorated Christmas trees, went to auctions together, took in movies on Forty-second Street, made love in fields, on beaches. Of course, that was before we had the children. (*in tears*) I hate losing him after all these years to that slob. (*catches sight of herself in the mirror*) My boobs are falling. I haven't a prayer!

COLLIN: Calm down, Lady. Leonard's forty-five. That's all that's wrong with him. He's afraid he'll die and miss something.

BLAIR: (*tears a comb through her hair*) Call me by my right name, damn it! I'm not *Lady*. I'm a scorned, hysterical wife who's going to ruin this performance. And don't you dare defend him! He's no better than a bull. Chasing every heifer in the field. (*She grabs her purse and takes out a bag of Snickers. She gobbles one.*)

COLLIN: You'll get fat eating those. I'll buy you a sandwich. How about roast beef?

BLAIR: Shove your sandwich! And don't look at me like that. I'm not suicidal … like you!

COLLIN: I gave up suicide.

BLAIR: No, you just take drugs. That's what the children say. You think that's the answer? Shooting up your arm with God knows what?

COLLIN: You can't prove that!

BLAIR: No, it's just a guess. You're so placid lately. At least your boyfriends don't run off on *you*.

COLLIN: (*offended*) I don't have boyfriends. Where'd you get that idea?

BLAIR: (*eats more chocolate*) Come off it, Collin. You're gay. Why hide it? Can't you see we couldn't care less what you are? I was in love with Monty Clift when I was young, and *he* was gay. Anyway … if I tried suicide, the union would suspend me. Equity'd put me on probation, and I'd never act again. (*tries to smile*)

COLLIN: You shouldn't joke about serious things like suicide or being gay. (*nastily*) Your teeth are brown. You'd better rinse your mouth before going onstage. (*abruptly switches subject*) Leonard should be on his way home soon. I phoned this afternoon and told him you were raving. Leonard probably took Air Sunshine to Miami and then, when he got to Miami, he'd connect with Delta. When he gets to New York—if he left his car at the airport—he'll drive straight here.

BLAIR: Stop that travelogue! Get yourself some dinner and leave me alone.

(*Watching him walk away, she sits and eats her candy grimly.*)

Entry Thirteen

꩜ When Collin left, I stayed at my dressing table and reflected on Leonard's lies. He had done so many numbers on my head, I figured I had been imagining Laurie's presence loitering in our lives. I was glad I had found out the truth, that my intuition wasn't just a figment of a jealous nature. John was right; jealousy doesn't kill. I got up, rinsed out my mouth and adjusted my costume with pride. No matter what, I was going to survive. I went onstage, and did what I was trained to do. ꩜

(*She goes off and completes her performance.* Collin *watches in the wings as she bows. He imitates her, then applauds along with the phantom audience. He calls to her, "Lady!"*)

COLLIN: He's here. He's in the parking lot and wants to see you.

93

⌒ When I put my street clothes on, I went out the stage door, Collin walking ahead of me as if he were paving the way for a shell-shocked victim. We slid along the side of the theater building. Leonard, in the parking lot, looked concerned. I made a beeline straight for the car, ignoring him. I was afraid if he said a word to me, I'd either faint or hit him across the face. I did that once, and he hit me back. I climbed in the front seat. ⌒

LEONARD: (*walks over to her, speaks gently*) Get out of the car. Come in MY car ... Will you ride with me, please?

BLAIR: (*turns away*) Don't touch me! I don't want to look at you! I don't want to drive home with you.

LEONARD: I came all the way back to talk to you. Down and up in one day. (*pulls up a chair and sits next to her*) Collin said you were hysterical. What's wrong? What did you hear? Whatever it is, it isn't true.

BLAIR: Why did you do it?

LEONARD: Do what?

BLAIR: Get involved with that floozy. (*pleading*) Was it my fault? Was I so unreachable? Leonard, why didn't you say something? If you went to bed with her, you did it to be mean. Payback time. Just like Collin. You guys are tearing me apart.

LEONARD: (*acting confused*) I don't know what you're talking about, Blair. All I wanted was a quiet weekend in the Keys, alone.

BLAIR: (*ignoring his lie*) This is all about my ambition,

isn't it? Leonard, I need to act! That's what I *do!* Why must you punish me for it? What do I have to do to work, and keep you faithful?

LEONARD: I *am* faithful, Blair. You're imagining this. Who told you what?

BLAIR: You bastard! Collin … Joanie. The airline tickets. You charged two, not one. And you told her she could buy a bathing suit? Down *there,* for crying out loud!

LEONARD: Are you going nuts? I *had* to cancel your unused ticket, I charged mine. We made a new rule in the office, remember? Everyone has to pay for spouse travel out-of-pocket. What lies have you been listening to … and bought?

BLAIR: Obviously not yours.

LEONARD: Can you hear yourself? You sound like that dyke in the play.

BLAIR: (*heatedly*) That's right, Leonard. Go ahead, accuse *me* the way you do every time *you're* in the wrong.

LEONARD: (*gently pulling her closer*) It feels wrong to me, too. All of it. You're difficult, Blair. You really are. You believe everything you hear. You're oversensitive. And it wouldn't be surprising if I *did* bring someone with me, because … oh, what the hell. You don't even feel yourself moving away from me, do you? So engrossed, so inaccessible.

BLAIR: Don't confuse me! What am I to believe? Does that mean you're guilty and lying and punishing me, or am I just going mad?

LEONARD: Why is someone always doing something to

you? What about the children ... me? (*looks around at the theater parking lot*) Did it ever occur to you that I would like to be able to afford to express myself again? To direct, or act or *something!* Be involved with something besides real estate? I admit I'm jealous of you doing this play. Not you doing it, just that you're having fun while I'm breaking my neck to make a buck. Have some compassion, Blair. The world doesn't start and end with you. But my world does ... (*his voice breaks*)

BLAIR: (*abashed*) Poor Leonard. Poor me. I'm not very understanding, am I? I suppose if you went back to theater, were acting again ... I still would find a reason to worry. To feel insecure about you. People like Joanie and Collin ... they're bearers of bad tidings, aren't they?

LEONARD: They don't count. We do. Our marriage does. The truth is, we have to give each other more space, more trust. Try to think of our marriage as something that needs protecting, more than me and more than you.

BLAIR: Other people make their marriages work. But how do mates hear these terrible, hurtful things about each other, and still believe, have faith? We're both so vulnerable. (*sighs*) You go ahead, I'll go with Collin. I don't feel like riding with you just yet. What a luxury it would be, if we both could go back to the stage. (*He turns and exits, she looks after him.*) If we don't destroy each other first.

↜ Leonard came back to me, guilty or not. What did it matter? The sum total of us was the marriage. He didn't speak to Collin for a month, and I didn't speak to Joanie for longer than that. I thought, who needs enemies with those two around?

We both nursed our marriage back to health. I was so happy when we moved down to Fairfield County, about ninety miles closer to New York City. Instead of two years, we had actually stayed in Falls Village almost ten.

Suddenly, my father passed away, and I became an heiress. I missed him more than I ever dreamed. Even our children were rich, although we tried to raise them as if they were not, for their own sakes. I inherited industrial property in Stamford, and Leonard was eager to help manage it. It was important that we live close by. I like to think my father would have been pleased. How I wished I could hear his strident voice again, insisting that I go downstairs and play in the fresh air! My father died of a heart attack, frantically reaching for the doorknob. I wonder where he was heading that was so terribly urgent?

My mother became a serene, elegant widow, managing quite well with the help of Oscar and Anna. She got rid of my father's Oriental rugs. She thought they looked shabby. Anything decaying depressed her. Mother was a wall-to-wall carpet person, a product of Albany, New York, who spent her youth around the corner from State Street and the local tennis courts. My father used to call her small-town. I fought that reputation like the plague, and so did Joanie, who was born in Queens.

Joanie didn't stay in Queens long. New York City was just as necessary for her as it had been for me.

The most significant things about Joanie were her large hazel eyes, her blond-streaked hair and ready laugh. She also was noted for her gigantic bosom and love of men—most men, in fact. She was twice divorced and many times bedded down. A cantankerous extrovert, but fun, she didn't think highly of Collin.

My cousin, who was anything but plain, made fun of my mother as if she were her own. Mother was more beautiful than Joanie. Mother was dark and attractive, with a certain childishness and naiveté that clung to her. Joanie said that everything about my mother was safe and middle-class—"just like her wall-to-wall carpeting."

On the contrary, Joanie was so assertive, men called her a ball-breaker. Her second husband had tried to push her over the ship's railing on their honeymoon.

When I married and left home, life changed. Marriage was not what it was cracked up to be. But my theater interests already had set me miles apart from my mother or Joanie, with her man-hunting. I was different in many ways. When I was an aspiring actress, I had a poster of Leda's Swan in my room. Mother had a Utrillo over her mantel. On the walls of my first married quarters, theater posters hung. One was of me in the arms of an actor. The play was by Molière. I had often appeared in classics. The print read, "Starring Blair Neville, directed by Leonard Stewart." I was true to my dream and, in our early years, so was he. ⇐

Entry Fourteen

⌒ I'm not so sure I liked myself, the way I appeared in my journal. But if you couldn't expose yourself in all lights in your own journal, where could you?

It came easily, putting my thoughts into dialogue and scenes, after so many years of theater. The trouble with reading most journals or diaries is that you can see the world through only one person's perspective. Writing scenes allowed me to imagine Leonard or Collin speaking just as I knew they would, giving their own viewpoints. It kept me from contemplating to excess my own navel.

This way, Blair became another character, no longer I, myself. It had a wonderful effect, giving me much-needed and useful distance from the scenes that really happened. I liked this distance, especially when life became so ugly, close up. It seemed logical, that if you transformed grief, concentrated on getting bad times down on paper as literally as you could, you could make yourself feel those things happened to someone else. They became philosophical problems seen from a safer vantage point. I really hoped I might eliminate the pain that memory brought—banish sadness, twist life like a wet mop and drip the residue onto the printed page.

The way I wrote my journal had to be more helpful than talking to a therapist like Doctor Faber the Silent, whom I had tried in New York the week before the children, Leonard and I left for Falls Village.

I flipped through the journal pages and read: "Doctor Faber—lord of mutedom, master of indifference."

I went to see the therapist the afternoon before my thirty-third birthday. I didn't want to be in his waiting room that day. The weather was too hot and sultry. I should have been sitting on the grass outside a barn in some stock company, waiting for my cue. But you can't function when you are as hysterical as I felt then.

Faber didn't believe in air conditioning. Finally, when I went into his office, the doctor seemed too aloof to be interested in what I had to say. I tried to stop myself, but couldn't, and a torrent of words burst out. ⌐

BLAIR: Doctor, I hate my life! I hate being a wife and I hate being a mother. I hate cooking and washing and taking the children to school. My eight-year-old son pees behind the radiator in the stairwell of the apartment house. The retriever poops all over the floor, and Leonard won't clean it. I have to do all the dirty work. I shouldn't be stuck like this, for God's sake. I should be on the stage! That's what I was trained for.

(Dr. Faber *hands her a tissue.* Blair *nods "thank you" and proceeds.*)

BLAIR: When I drive out of town, I see sports cars racing by on the highway, and I fall in love with every driver. I see a man's elbow on the open car window ahead of me, and I want him to stop and get out and make a pass at me, to make love to me, if you want to know the truth. Who wants to grow up? I hate seeing the names of my successful friends crop up in the newspapers, friends who don't have children. I hate filling out school forms, so the kids'll grow up and turn into what Leonard and I've become … has-beens in our thirties.

Doctor, in Falls Village, I'll be standing still. I hate all my friends who seem to have their artistic careers pulled together better than we do! I spurned businessmen years ago to marry an actor. Now he's turning into a businessman! He tricked me! Upstate Connecticut's the end of the world. And Leonard is all excited about Litchfield County. He's determined to move there, a lot farther even than Stamford, where my father has his main office. I used to think *that* was the sticks. I'll go bats if we move to Falls Village! It'll be worse than my parents' beach house, where Leonard watches ball games all weekend, and I'm so bored I help Anna polish silver and wash floors. A college educated woman like me washing floors? I can't wait to get back to the city! Now I'll get here about once a year.

(*no answer*)

(*exasperated*) You never say a word! You've got to help me. Doctor, I'm cracking up! Did you ever see *A Streetcar Named*

Desire? Well, like Blanche Dubois, I feel like I'm in a trap. I want to run away. But run to where? I came home with my suitcase one time, and my mother sent me back. She said, "You made your bed; now lie in it." So where do I go from here, and what do I do?

(Dr. Faber *sighs and then exits, shaking his head and leaving* Blair *sitting there.*)

༄ He never answered me. I came back once more. He never answered me then, either, like most men. And that sums up my experience with therapists. I turned to my journal. That was my therapy. Collin took drugs when he felt trapped. He believed he was in control of his destiny. I was far too smart to think that.

It's great to pretend to be in charge of your life. On paper, it's easy to make choices. On paper you can force your characters to change, to resolve their problems. No doctor could do that for me. Later, I discovered that reality is only what we *do,* and what happens in the very next instant. Forget about resolution! There is no resolution. In plays, or otherwise. And, consequently, there is no blame. I've come to realize that blame is a word we threw around a lot for years, a senseless/useless word. It felt as if Leonard, Collin and I created the word, "blame." Leonard used it most. He frustrated me. In fact, I hoped that after writing all this down, the frustration would evaporate, like mist in sunlight.

I understand that life is, by its very nature, something that changes by the instant, changes as suddenly as the moon on occasion eclipses the sun. What stays the same is the story, trapped on paper, trapped in thought. Could it be that one writes to hold on to events and feelings? This record of my time with Leonard and Collin might prove to be a way to hold on to all those years that, in retrospect, were rewarding as well as contentious.

The special times of our young marriage flood back and back again, as I read over my journal. Maybe I haven't got it right. Maybe I just want to gather up the pain of all those days, like a bouquet of Collin's spring flowers. Maybe it's more bittersweet than that: to combine the twinges of pleasure, twinges of regret. All the dark deeds, all the sweet songs. Write it down in an effort to make the conclusions less skewed, more understandable. And by the very effort of fictionalizing, trying to force every conflict to come out right in the end … which, in real life, of course, it never does. ⌒

 Entry Fifteen

⌒ It used to be a matter of honor with me that I never invaded Collin's privacy. By now, he had squeezed halfway out of the closet. He didn't deny he was gay, didn't talk about marrying a sweet "chick" or "broad" someday. Of course, John had been right. Besides, Collin didn't want to marry anyone. He wanted to stay with us. He wanted to keep our homes shipshape, to scour and polish and plant at that snail's pace of his and stay a part of our family. By now, he was an undisputed member.

We were in the kitchen, the day I nearly gutted Collin with a knife. ↢

(Collin *enters. He stands at the sink, ready to prepare another meal.* Blair *joins him. She watches as* Collin *dices vegetables slowly, then puffs on his pipe. He alternates: puff, cut, puff, cut.* Blair *trembles in frustration as he begins delicately to tear the lettuce.*)

B L A I R: (*voice subdued, teeth gritted*) Please—don't—do—that.

C O L L I N: (*innocently*) Do what?

B L A I R: (*controlling an urge to remove his eyeballs*) Tear that lettuce into tiny, little pieces. Wash and dry each leaf. Chop like that. We'll starve before you're finished!

C O L L I N: (*breezily*) You do it your way, I'll do it mine.

B L A I R: Here, let me!

C O L L I N: (*watching*) You're going to hurt yourself. That knife's sharp.

B L A I R: (*zip, zip, zip ... tear, tear, tear ...*) See! It's done! On to the broiled pork chops ... oh damn! (*Cuts finger.* Collin *smothers a grin.*)

C O L L I N: If you had been more careful ...

B L A I R: (*Deadly quiet, she holds the knife pointed at him.*

Speaks between clenched lips.) Not one word! Not one single, wretched word!

COLLIN: (*unconcerned, fishes in his pocket*) Here's a Band-Aid. Let me wrap your finger. A hasty movement causes hurt, / when the cook is not alert.

BLAIR: (*wildly furious*) Your poetry never scans! (*She accepts Band-Aid and puts it on.*)

COLLIN: I made brownies for dessert.

BLAIR: You know where you can shove them.

(*She starts out of the kitchen door, then stops. She is tempted by a plate of brownies. Furtively, she looks around, then grabs one. Collin sees her, their eyes lock.*)

BLAIR: (*mocking*) I keep forgetting this is your pièce de résistance. Forgive me and I'll forgive you. Or does your salad speak for you?

COLLIN: *Oui,* the salad, *c'est moi.* It's fresher and chopped better than those at the Marriott. I know the chef. He lives up on High Ridge. You know ... near that gas station that chiseled us? You remember. You had the Bentley then. The one Leonard bought, with the faulty brakes. I drove you around at Christmas in the city ...

BLAIR: (*laughing*) And never looked behind you when you pulled out in traffic. You finish the salad. I'd bleed all over it.

COLLIN: I forgive you. Take a Valium.

(Leonard *enters and smiles, watching them, out of their line of sight* Blair *looks at* Collin *as he tears the lettuce, at a slightly faster pace.*)

LEONARD: Two brats in the same sandbox.

⟅ Not long after that, I had a much worse accident.

One particular evening, when Leonard was away as usual, and I wasn't rehearsing or performing, I decided to take a shower upstairs, in our bathroom. As I stepped out of the stall, Ophelia, the peekapoo, brushed between my legs, begging for attention. I lost my balance, fell and cracked my head on the ceramic tiles Leonard paid such a fortune to install. There was a lot of blood and my ankle was twisted. The bathroom was tilting, and I was as dazed as if I'd been drunk. At first, I didn't realize the blood was coming from my head. I couldn't stand up, so I screamed and screamed. ⟅

(Blair *lies curled up on the floor.* Collin *enters and sees her. He gasps.*)

BLAIR: (*dizzy, disoriented*) Collin … Help me.

COLLIN: Oh my God. There's blood all over. Shall I run to the pharmacy for … some sanitary napkins?

BLAIR: Don't you *dare* leave! Call for help, Collin. Quickly! I'm blacking out! Get the police.

COLLIN: You don't need the police! I hate the police! You'll be all right. You've had this bleeding before. Here's your robe.

BLAIR: It's my *head,* you idiot! I fell! You want me to die here? Call 911.

COLLIN: (*hesitates*) They'll think I raped you.

BLAIR: The hell they will. I'll tell them you're gay. Do as I say, damn it! Call for an ambulance or you'll be responsible if I die. I'm bleeding to death, Collin. Hurry … (*closes her eyes, leans back, and starts to sob*)

COLLIN: All right. (*goes into bedroom, picks up receiver and punches the keys slowly*) Let's see … 9-1-1. A good day to you too, officer. The lady I work for is lying in a pool of blood. No, no one killed her. She's still alive. Where do we live? It's Greenwich, 1500 Warwick Way. It's the big house with the hemlock trees and the white picket fence that needs painting. I plan to get to that next month.

BLAIR: (*screams from the bathroom floor*) Collin, you're a dead man!

COLLIN: She wants an ambulance fast. You better not cross her, officer. She's mean as a snake. (*hangs up and returns to bathroom*)

BLAIR: Get some towels. O-h-h.

COLLIN: They have your monogram on them. The blood won't come out, unless, of course, you use Woolite mixed with Comet. Maybe paper towels would be better.

BLAIR: (*moans*) Oh, my God! Get help! Run downstairs. Find a neighbor. Get a grown-up to help me. A sane person.

COLLIN: The ambulance is on the way. I'll meet the EMTs outside and bring them up here. (*He runs out.*)

✍ He did call a neighbor, and the police came and took me to Emergency, where they finally stopped the bleeding. I had thirty-five stitches, fortunately on the back of my head where it wouldn't show when the hair grew back. The fact is, he *did* save my life, in spite of his confusion. I don't think that surprised anyone as much as it did him. Now, no matter how crazy he could be … how could I ever forget a thing like that?

Bit by bit, my head healed. How could you feel glamorous with a bandaged head? Now I needed Collin more than ever. Leonard saw that, too. He was very grateful for the way Collin took care of me. It let *him* off the hook.

That was a low point in my life. Again, I let go of my shaky career. Gave up acting, concentrated on my journal and began writing stories. At least I could do that at home. Leonard was pleased. He could report to me everything that was going on with the Stamford properties my father had willed me. The children were in college, by then. Kay had inherited enough money to buy a small weekend retreat near a guru, who claimed she was a 400-year-old warrior. Kay was simultaneously in love with a girl and a boy, whose names I can't recall. ↬

COLLIN: She should make up her mind which sex she prefers.

BLAIR: That took *you* forty years.

↫ Weekends, Kay went to her retreat to chant and live a natural life. Spirituality was running rampant. I was on a health kick, building my body with yoga and exercise. Mark had been working at the Board of Realtors for the summer. He had set up such a fine computer system that now he was out of a job. This didn't faze him one bit, because he had been studying Zen and nothing mattered except existing for the moment, or so he told me. He had fallen in love, amazingly, with a member of the opposite sex. He was following in my footsteps; he was attending Bennington, too.

Finally, I had Collin and Leonard to myself: a mixed blessing, admittedly. But, while my married friends were trying to find good household help and my single women friends were complaining how hard it was to find a man, I had Leonard in my bed and Collin in the kitchen and garden, serving a life sentence. ✑

 *Entry Sixteen*

✑ The children grew to be strong and independent. They were experimental and liberal, while Collin retained the bigotry of the insecure.

One morning, Collin came out of the kitchen, his hot coffee and no one else's in hand, complaining, grumbling really, as he loped through the swinging door. ✑

COLLIN: I read Kay's letter. She shouldn't be running around with riffraff. What's she hanging around niggers for?

BLAIR: Who do you mean, riffraff? Cindy's an educated young woman and Kay's roommate.

COLLIN: (*turning down his lips*) You probably didn't even realize that coon's a dyke!

LEONARD: Why are you using those ugly words? That's pretty low-class.

COLLIN: This family's too important to be messing around with a black phys ed major.

BLAIR: You don't know anything about Cindy. And you've got one hell of an imagination about her sex life. I never want to hear you condemn sexual preference or race. Keep your prejudices to yourself. I can't believe you'd insult Kay's friends. We taught her to be open-minded, which is more than you are.

COLLIN: She's a lucky girl. She should be learning to be a leader. (*retreats*)

BLAIR: (*calls after him*) You can be a lesbian *and* a leader.

LEONARD: Do you think Cindy's really a lesbian? How would Collin know?

BLAIR: I wouldn't worry. Even if she is, what could we do about it? What Kay does at school is her business, not ours.

↪ Nevertheless, as Collin indicated, we were lucky. Mother told me, when I was a child, that many people were starving everywhere and that I must value my own good fortune. She knew we could make a difference in the world.

I think children who are born rich often wonder why they're

so blessed. I mean, you are given many comforts and pretty things and life is easier than it is for most, but surely you're not put on this planet merely to acquire or to gratify yourself. In short, I believe if you're not careful, having money can rob you of both incentive and normalcy. Mother guarded against that. She urged me to do my best. My father *demanded* it.

So I've always pushed myself. I pursued a career and tried to help finance major causes. I gave to the endowment fund of my college and donated to Planned Parenthood. There was to be a clinic named after me. The ceremony was scheduled, and we all were thrilled.

It was a fine day near the end of summer. Collin followed Leonard and me up the stairs of the paint-chipped, gray wooden building on Washington Boulevard that housed the local headquarters of Planned Parenthood. A new metal plaque leaning in the window bore my name, "Blair Neville Stewart." Just spotting it made me proud.

"Watch the cracks with those high heels," warned Leonard. He turned to Collin, who stood gawking at several picketers. On the sidewalk, two women and a man in a checkered shirt bore a placard that read, "Babies Have No Choice."

Leonard said, "Revolting exploitation of sentiment. Come on, Collin. Hurry up. There are a dozen people here already."

Collin tripped over the first step. "I don't like to cross picket lines," he said.

"You're pro-choice, what are you talking about? You'd better be or what are you doing here?" I snapped.

"Accompanying you," he said. "That pink print looks great on you."

We three entered the waiting room, where the cocktail party honoring my substantial donation was in progress. I was greeted by enthusiastic applause.

Let me mention how Collin looked that day. He was dressed in chinos and a white shirt open at the throat, revealing the kind of paisley ascot Leonard wore to formal functions when he wanted to play British lord. On Collin's head was that old black Greek sailor's cap with the duck bill. Both items were picked up on one of his trips abroad. I knew that cap was glued on, so to speak. He'd never remove it, inside the house, or out. Collin appeared pleased with himself. He liked hobnobbing with "classy people," as he called them. He carried himself carefully, a man of distinction. His shoes shone, and his fingernails were so clean, you'd never take him for a gardener.

Maude Lawrence and her assistant, Pat, talked to me after the formal part of the ceremony had ended. ⌐

MAUDE: (*enthusiastically*) We are all so pleased to be getting this windfall from you at a time when *Roe v. Wade* is in jeopardy.

PAT: (*drink in hand*) We enjoyed you so much when we saw you onstage in Tarrytown. Wonderful that you've extended your interest to women's matters. We're thrilled to be recipients.

BLAIR: Pat, it's *my* pleasure. You're the generous one. So

brave, the way you work in this organization, no matter what the outside interference.

PAT: Pro-lifers threaten us in the streets, sometimes. The picketing is potentially dangerous, I suppose.

BLAIR: I noticed a few today. Actually, I see them almost every time I drive past here.

PAT: (*shrugging*) We pay them little mind. Such violence in the world. Too many people. Too many have-nots. We do worry about that.

COLLIN: (*preening, basking in the glow of her notoriety*) The lady always cares about women. She feels sick when she reads about women being abused.

MAUDE: (*looking at Collin with interest*) And who is this, may I ask?

BLAIR: This is Collin Williams. (*hesitates, searching for a proper introduction*) Our associate.

COLLIN: (*tries to be modest and supercilious at the same time*) That's Collin, with two "els".

PAT: It's nice to have you here, Collin. You seem to be the only single man in the room.

MAUDE: (*passing him the tray of cheese balls*) You're like my late husband. He never minded being with a group of women, either.

LEONARD: Collin's a mystery man.

MAUDE: (*intrigued*) What do you mean, mystery man?

BLAIR: Well, Collin sort of wandered out of the rain into our lives and has stayed for fifteen years. Right, Leonard?

LEONARD: (*stares at* Collin, *who is eating all the cheese balls on the tray*) Our lives haven't been the same since the era of Collin began. By the way, he's quite the world traveler.

MAUDE: (*eagerly presenting* Collin *with a fresh tray of canapés*) Have you ever been to Capri, Collin? My husband and I used to go there.

COLLIN: (grinning widely) Did you know the hydrofoil from Naples to Capri travels as fast as an airplane? There is nothing like the isle of Capri,/ so much romance, so much to see. Just a rhyme I made up on the spur of the moment.

MAUDE: (*taken back, but still game*) How well informed you are! As a matter of fact, I have some travel folders in my office. My vacation comes up in September, so I soon have to decide where to go.

COLLIN: I collect those, too. Maybe I can give you some advice. I have folders on every ship that sails and all the major flights to Europe. The lady here says I'm a regular walking atlas. (*pauses, puffs on his pipe*) Traveling alone isn't as bad as they think. You can meet lots of people. Not just tourists, either. September's a good time to go to Italy. That's after the tourists clear out.

MAUDE: I can't get over how much you and I think alike. (*They wander off.*)

PAT: How wonderful! Maude has found an eligible man, thanks to you.

(Leonard *and* Blair *exchange meaningful glances.*)

LEONARD: (*shakes his head*) Poor Maude.

Entry Seventeen

⤸ Leonard thought I complained too much about Collin. ⤸

LEONARD: You're not the easiest to please, Blair. You're right, though. With Collin, there are plenty of valid aggravations. His disposition isn't always sunny. In fact, it can be dour.

BLAIR: God forbid you should try to hurry him. Collin becomes frantic, or furious when he doesn't get his own way. He also fibs. By the time the fibs grow into lies, it's too late. I'm too dependent on him.

LEONARD: We've overlooked lots of things. We ignore Collin's brooding, his wild shifts of mood. But then, we're ALL moody. You shouldn't pretend you're not, Blair.

BLAIR: Like when am I moody?

LEONARD: Moody AND bossy. Oh, I admit you're intelligent. But, if everyone doesn't do things your way ... LOOK OUT! Then you forget your sweet, charming self and scream a lot.

BLAIR: (*loudly*) I don't scream! I never scream ... (*softer, realizing she has contradicted herself*) I may *yell.* Anyhow, it's only out of frustration. You and Collin always gang up on me. Are you sure you want to hang around me, Darling, if I'm so unsatisfactory? Don't you have a house to build or a girl to flirt with or a plane to fly?

LEONARD: Now that you mention it, I do! (*gets up and leaves*)

BLAIR: Leonard's being unfair. What about *his* moodiness? *And* ... as I said, he won't say what's wrong. He just does something evasive. He acts! He fires people ambiguously. Leonard's a bit of a coward. I watched him fire two men once, and his tone was so apologetic, neither of them understood. They showed up for work the following day.

✎ Where was I? Oh, yes. I was becoming increasingly irritated with Leonard. Now that the Rhode Island project was finished, when he wasn't out of town on some mysterious errand, he would stay home, restlessly making phone calls and pacing the floor, spilling his coffee and messing up the desk in the library. By four o'clock, his aura filled the whole house. I couldn't think straight with him around.

The reasons I never wanted to get rid of Collin were numerous, not just because it's hard to hire a new person. It wasn't only fear of a stranger. The point is, I felt comfortable with Collin. His chitchat was what I needed, the very day we met. I could tell he was fascinated with me, and that's hard to resist.

There I was, stuck with Leonard bouncing off the walls, or off doing God knows what in the long beach grass, and me, for all intents and purposes, as good as married to Collin. Not involved sexually, you understand. But every other way. Between Leonard's disappearances and Collin, with his own moods and trips, and the children with their various romances, the devil was really getting his due. Well, I guess I'll get out my journal and write about it. ⌒

(Leonard *returns*.)

LEONARD: While you're at it, Blair, when you explain about me in your journal ... I hope you will write that no matter what I DID in life, what adventures I experienced, we always had a pact. We talked about it often. We said you should try everything ONCE. Whatever exploration I indulged in, was just that. That's the actor's motto, isn't it? Experiment! In spite of the way other people live their lives, we knew what we were doing. "Experience freedom," you said. So I did. That was something we agreed on in the beginning.

BLAIR: We agreed to nothing of the sort. At least, I didn't hear it that way! I had plenty of chances to fool around, but I didn't. Once an actor, always an actor! My father said they make rotten husbands.

LEONARD: Maybe I wasn't always faithful to the letter of our vows, but I was faithful to the spirit. (*tenderly*) You are now, and always have been, the love of my life. Don't you believe that?

BLAIR: I adore hearing you say it. Even if I don't always believe it. (*shrugs*) We all do things out of insecurity … And it's insecurity that drives you, Leonard. (*writes in her journal*) Leonard just loved to experiment, that's the truth in a nutshell. He has always had an incredible lust for life, and *that's* what came first with him. And maybe that's exactly what I loved most about him, though I'd never tell him that

LEONARD: You see me as insecure?

BLAIR: You're foolish to think otherwise.

LEONARD: I'm getting out while the getting's good. Too many revelations in one day. (*exits*)

BLAIR: (*writes*) Gone again. The truth is … I always admired Leonard's zest, and with it goes adventurousness. Like childhood diseases, like his "relationships," he'll recover. All I ever disliked were the lies; I understood the rest. The fact is, Leonard's kind and generous and romantic. He may not be there every time I need him, but how many women get romanced after twenty years of marriage? So many women never, ever experience romantic love in their lifetimes. Leonard's talent for romance counts for something, doesn't it?

✑ Still, not there is not there. I depended upon Collin. See, there must have been an element of destiny operating here. Because of Collin's faith in the mystical, I saw things differently. Our relationship seemed predestined … if you believed in karma. Collin did. Kay too. It was a subject I wouldn't have dared bring up with Leonard. He wasn't and never would be receptive. Too much of a realist.

But I was beginning to believe. Collin and I had a bond with one another that seemed to steer our lives. There must be experiences you're supposed to have, in order to grow. There are more things in heaven and earth than are dreamt of in your philosophy, my dear Horatio. So Hamlet said. Maybe Collin didn't just wander down the road that first day by accident or because of my fanciful pact with Lucifer. If there is such a thing as reincarnation, maybe our encounter was fated.

Searching my soul, I realized one reason I was so grateful for Collin's company was fear. I had learned how threatening it could be to take strangers into your house. But how could you be sure, at the beginning? Why, even the stranger you meet and marry is a stranger at first. Sooner or later you live together, and his influence on your life can be disastrous. I mean, how can you ever really tell? Answer: you can't! You can't tell if the people you choose to live with will make your life pleasant or painful. The bottom line: you can never be sure you are truly safe in your marriage, or in life. But when my marriage faltered, Collin was always there.

The truth is there isn't a minute that goes by when I see a flower in someone's garden or walk along a country road, or feel the crispness that ushers in a change of season, that I don't hear Collin's intake of breath, his exclamation of joy when there was beauty poking its colorful head up from the damp earth. There isn't a minute that goes by when I need to roast a turkey that I don't want to ask Collin how *he* would do it. I need to ask him how long to *cook* the bird and later, when my sweet tooth gets too bad, I need to ask him how many chocolate chips he used in the brownies. Just as I say, there isn't a moment that goes by that I don't feel the presence of Collin. I remember every little thing that happened to all of us. I can't get those events out of my mind. ↝

 Entry Eighteen

↜ A hysterectomy is a respectable operation. Women who have produced children are revered and remain so, even when their parts break down. I was a woman who had gone the distance, led a conventional life in some ways. Had children, *was* someone.

I had never exactly venerated the human body, although I exercised regularly. But I never liked the idea of someone cutting into me and removing anything. ↝

DR. EDELMAN: (*Enters and sits. He is fifty-something,*

balding, kindly, self-contained.) Why should you be afraid? The uterus is like a pit. After childbearing, a useless pit.

BLAIR: This is my body. *My* pit.

DR. EDELMAN: It's perfectly reasonable to have your uterus out. The organ isn't necessary, at your age.

BLAIR: I know several women who have gotten rid of theirs. They lost their virginity before I did, too. My friends always do everything first! Is it inevitable for me to lose mine?

DR. EDELMAN: (*chuckles quietly*) It's not really a question of losing anything. You still can enjoy intercourse. And you have two grown children. How do your friends feel now?

BLAIR: They were glad when it was over ... all the messiness, I mean.

DR. EDELMAN: So what are you worried about?

(*Watches him drawing on a pad. He doodles little fat circles.*)

⟜ I noticed the doctor was obsessed with pits. They looked like little wombs, those curlicues he was drawing. Of course, he wants to take it out. He gets paid ten thousand a womb. Besides, it's not *his* innards we're talking about. It's *my* pit he wants to tamper with, and I wasn't sure I was ready to let it go. After all, this womb had done me great service. It carried my children and conspired with my glands to give me sexual delight. They say, once it goes ... a whole era of your life is cut out. My poor body. My poor youth. Why have you deserted me? My womb gone. Youth gone; maybe pleasure gone, down the tubes. No pun intended.

I questioned Leonard at dinner. ✍

(Leonard *and* Collin *enter. They join* Blair.)

B L A I R : Pour the wine, Collin. It's already in the carafe.

C O L L I N : (*He pours himself a little wine and pompously takes a sip.*) An '81 Beaujolais. A truly moist grape, voluptuous, youthful and pregnant with the flavor of sensuality.

B L A I R : (*indignant*) Shut up, Collin! Your toast is obscene.

C O L L I N : (*hurt*) I was only trying to make you laugh.

L E O N A R D : (*soothingly*) My dearest, you will always be moist and voluptuous to me. And don't fuss at Collin. This isn't his fault. Sit down, Collin. Join us.

B L A I R : Oh, Leonard, I really don't know what to do. I hate the whole idea.

L E O N A R D : (*pours his own wine*) Get rid of it. Who cares? A woman's womb … what the hell use is it? I mean, we don't actually NEED it anymore, do we?

B L A I R : (*smiles lovingly at* Leonard) Oh no, Darling. We don't really need it. Thanks for being so aware, so sensitive. (*glares at* Collin, *who sits*)

C O L L I N : (*Chews his salad, while pieces of lettuce fall from the tip of his fork. He speaks with his mouth full.*) I think we should get it over with soon. I hate to watch you with those cramps each month.

B L A I R : What do you mean *we*, Kemo Sabe? I don't care *what* you think.

L E O N A R D : Let him say what he wants, Honey. He's eating at the same table, isn't he? Collin's one of the family.

BLAIR: Are we putting this to a vote? Whether I keep my uterus or not?

COLLIN: (*oblivious*) It's been nothing but an embarrassment. Isn't that so?

BLAIR: What *are* you talking about?

COLLIN: Remember what you said happened in London? Last year, on the twenty-first of January, wasn't it? The fog was as thick as soup. I drove you to Kennedy on Tuesday, and the traffic was interminable. One lane was closed. We would have been better off taking the Merritt Parkway, like I said. You were in a terrible mood. You had cramps then. And when you got back, you told us how you bled all over the bed at the Savoy. That really depressed you. You had to skip the theater. Haymarket, wasn't it?

LEONARD: (*to* Blair, *surprised*) Is nothing sacred?

BLAIR: You are disgusting, Collin. We're at dinner, for Christ's sake!! When I tell you personal things, I expect you to ignore the gory details. Not report them, as if you were an eye-witness on TV.

COLLIN: (*gets up indignantly and walks out*) I never ignore what you tell me. Sorry if you find that offensive.

BLAIR: Oh, damn. If he sulks, I'll have to do the dishes. (*calls after him*) I'm sorry I hurt your feelings, Collin. (*watches him go*) We're here all day talking together, he and I. Half the time I simply forget he's not one of my women friends.

LEONARD: (*calls out*) Collin, we're going in the other

room. (*to* Blair) We should discuss your physical condition in private.

BLAIR: So who invited him to join us? (*calls*) Collin, don't bother with dessert. Finish your dinner.

(*They stand there, waiting.* Collin *doesn't return. They look at one another.*)

LEONARD: Guess I'll do the dishes.

BLAIR: Guess I'll have the surgery.

↜ The fateful day arrived. I lay in the hospital bed the night before the operation, terrified. What if after this respectable operation, I might not be able to become aroused? Forty-five and no more feelings. Then a worse thought occurred to me. What if I died?

I said a prayer that night. Dear God, save me … I'm not ready for oblivion. I thought … no more of Collin's brownies and Leonard's caresses.

Later, the prepping, the intravenous. I watched Collin and Leonard wave and go down the hall. "Good night, good night," they said. They smiled, they waved. Two lovely boys. Cheerful. Why not? Everyone's happy when his stomach is full and he's well. They were well, *and* leaving. I thought how hard it is to be a woman.

The nurses knew. They fidgeted, comforted me, hung up the bottle that dripped into a needle they inserted in my arm. ↜

BLAIR: Finally, I'm alone. They've turned off the light in

my room, turned off the TV and the corridors are still, except for the tapping of the nurses' shoes on the rubberized tiles outside. I yearn for sleep. I want sleep desperately. The sooner asleep, the sooner sweet forgetfulness.

Come, sleep. As Juliet said, "Gallop apace, you fiery-footed steeds, … and bring in cloudy night immediately." I have rarely had trouble with sleep before. I don't want to look at this dark, friendless room any longer. I miss the odor of Collin's pipe. Who would have believed it?

Sleep is not my friend tonight. I lie here thinking that they are actually going to poke me with more needles and dab me with swabs of cotton; with drugs, reduce me to a state of infancy; insert a knife into my flesh and pinch me with clamps.

Lying in this bed helpless, in what seems like a warped cradle, I think of Leonard. How I love him, faults and all. The bed has metal sides that pen me in, guard me from falling. An infant's bed. Mother, where are you? Leonard, where are you? The rabbi said, for better or worse … You better come back right now, Leonard, damn it, and see if they're treating your bride right.

Leonard, do you hear me? You were there when the womb was new. Where are you now?

꙰ Morning dawned, quiet, soothing, gray. Someone was calling me. ꙰

NURSE: Mrs. Stewart, are you awake? We're taking you for

a little ride.

BLAIR: Where's my shot?

NURSE: Here it comes, Sweetie. Most of it's in you already.

⌐ I watched the bottle swing to and fro. Two giant football players in green came toward me, shifted me into a big baby carriage and rolled me down the hall. I tried to climb out, right in the middle of that bright hallway where they left me. I planned to escape but they strapped me down. Sadists! You'll get yours, I longed to shout. I think, cut me up into little stars, and I'll make the face of heaven so fine … Better stars in the sky to light the way for young lovers, the way Juliet requested, than death by operating room.

The green-masked monsters kept appearing and staring at me, telling me everything was all right. What did *they* know?

Then, *he* suddenly arrived, the lower part of his face covered. He was holding a black ether mask with a tube on the end. This was it! I was going to be smothered. ⌐

ANESTHESIOLOGIST: How you doing, Mrs. Stewart? Just relax. I'm going to help you sleep. You ever go to Fire Island? I just bought a house there. Sixty grand. Can you beat that? Some bargain. Mrs. Stewart, can you hear me?

BLAIR: (*thinks aloud*) He's indifferent to the fact that they will soon be carving away at me as if I were Thanksgiving dinner. How cruel illness is. How inhuman, when you can't speak, lose control. Just a thing, covered with a sheet. No one cares about this soul or mind. Chop chop, get the rubbery thing out. What am I to him but a mortgage payoff?

↪ Too late to cry out. He put the mask over my mouth and nose. I counted backward, too scared not to comply, then I was out. I was asleep when I was wheeled out of the operating room, soon to awaken. ↪

(*A nurse pats* Blair's *shoulder and stands back.*)

BLAIR: (*sleepily*) How insignificant illness makes us all.

(Collin *enters the hospital room. He bears a small bouquet of flowers.*)

COLLIN: Bet you're glad it's over. Leonard's downstairs buying more flowers. Mine are camellias. More distinctive than the ones he'll pick out, like the daffodils you saw in the field with your mother on the way to the Barrows Hotel, when you were a kid. Oh, I remember, all right. We drove there once. That's before you make that turnoff to the Belt Parkway. These are a wonderful pink color, don't you think? I bought them at Bull's Head. There's a place called Exotica at the intersection of Washington and Summer. (*seeing her face*) Can I get you anything?

BLAIR: (*weakly*) Is it really over?

COLLIN: You need makeup. I never realized you have those little broken blood vessels next to your nose.

BLAIR: (*after a moment*) What did they do with *it*?

COLLIN: (*baffled*) Do with what?

B L A I R : (*groggy*) The pit … the *thing*.

C O L L I N : (*fondly*) She's hysterical. (*to nurse*) See, she's an actress. They imagine things. Sometimes she lets me be an extra. We did *Caesar and Cleopatra* in Sharon. I was a slave. She beat me with the cat-o'-nine-tails. It was the proudest moment of my life, being on stage with the lady. (*leans over* Blair *and salaams*) Your wish is my command, O Pharaoh's Daughter.

B L A I R : (*coming back to life*) That'll be the day!

↜ Leonard came in, told me he loved me and asked if I were tired. Then he bent over and kissed me and before the drugs wore off, again said he loved me and that everything was fine. Later, at home, my sense of relief was immense. My poor, shocked body woke up and functioned again. I started reading New Age literature and tried to fill myself with a pride in my own being, trying to gain enough faith to get on with those middle years and the good life that was yet to come. ↜

Entry Nineteen

↜ After Leonard taught him to drive, Collin totaled our station wagon out of sheer nervousness. He grew jittery when he drove. But after he practiced and acquitted himself with our various wagons and sedans, I let him use mine. A few months before I went into the hospital, we replaced it with a BMW.

Collin was thrilled. He loved that car. We got him into the habit of driving me into New York to visit friends or to take classes at the New School on West Twelfth Street. Studying play writing was a wonderful way to recuperate from surgery.

Sometimes I took Collin out to lunch on the way back from the city. People would look at us across the dining room of the Chinese restaurant I liked off York Avenue. Lord, how I hated to have people think Collin was my husband! It was his gawkiness and that idiotic grin. I hate my own vanity, but it's there. Passed down from my mother, no doubt. Well, Collin didn't fit the husband role, which was not surprising. He thought he resembled a squire with that Greek cap and his pipe-smoking affectation. Always puffing away. Leonard and I could never stand smokers. For some reason, we let Collin smoke, because he seemed to have so little else in life, and because we hoped he was just smoking regular tobacco.

Collin used to drive me to the airport and, at times, his chatter aggravated me. He made me wild, gabbing on and on about "our dog" and "our house" and "our gardens." The retriever, killed by a truck before we left Falls Village, had long ago been replaced by Ophelia. Puck, a Lhasa Apso, was a new addition, housebroken by Collin's slow, steady persistence. Looking out the car window, Collin would say, "Hey, Lady, look at that cute one. Just like our Puck."

"Keep your eyes on the road," I'd reply.

And Collin's *driving!* He was a tailgater and a brake-jammer. When he drove, I couldn't look and I couldn't listen. I sat there tuning him out, fantasizing about the exotic places I used to go before I was married, and the world out there with the attractive men I used to date, pre-childbearing, pre-Connecticut, away from the company of this blabbermouth, who was playing bumper tag with my life. I let him go on and on, because I never meant to insult him.

When Collin himself traveled, his spirit lifted. He prepared for each trip as if it were a welcome career change. He wrote me postcards. When he came back, he brought more books to add to his collection of junk and memorabilia that filled the boxes in his basement apartment. After he would return from a trip, there was all hell to pay. Collin sank into black moods. ⌣

(Collin *enters and sits at the kitchen table.* Blair *joins him.*)

COLLIN: I don't know what there is to live for. I'm nothing. My job is nothing.

BLAIR: You want to take courses, maybe, at night? You could prepare, so you could work for the airlines. If worse came to worse, I could get another helper if you really wanted to leave.

COLLIN: (*bitterly*) I couldn't do that!

BLAIR: Why not?

COLLIN: (*matter-of-factly*) Because I can't, that's why. No, I think I'll just kill myself! Hang myself!

BLAIR: We're into that again! Don't kill yourself when I'm out buying groceries. I don't want Leonard coming home and finding your body dangling from the chandelier.

⮑ At first I was terrified when he made those threats. But after he refused psychological help, I became disgusted and mocked him. ⮑

BLAIR: Collin, just go away and do whatever you have to do to pull yourself out of this depression.

COLLIN: Oh, all right. If you don't care, why should I? I'm going to weed the garden now.

BLAIR: (*relieved*) Sounds good to me. That should cheer you up. Just don't drown the pansies or mutilate the lilacs.

(Collin *skulks off.*)

⮑ I realize his behavior was partially a bid for attention. At the time, I simply tried to make him get his anger out in the open, instead of allowing him to submerge himself in self-pity. Depression is rage turned inward. I tried to turn it outward. Eventually, Collin would forget about it and go to a movie, or read a book on railroads and became engrossed in some locomotive. Better still, boats were his favorite. He could forget his troubles by contemplating pictures of the *Queen Mary* and recounting tales of his crossing, when a Mrs. Henshaw took him for a gentleman of leisure and flirted with him the whole nine-day trip.

Collin recounted to me all his old trips, and time moved on. Things were peaceful until the thieving began. I was disconcerted by missing money, misplaced jewelry.

And so it started, the trouble, the questions and the locked drawers. I bought a closet safe and speculated upon who was doing what. By now I had decided Collin was right to lock his door.

But who was stealing? Could it be the children's college friends? Surely not. The workmen helping with our various remodelings? They charged so much, I figured they had stolen enough. Collin insisted he and his visitors weren't into booze or dope, at that time, and I wanted to believe him. Collin was spending more and more time in his apartment in the basement. I felt a grown man should have privacy. But I wondered if maybe the young guys who dropped in when Collin was off-duty were responsible for my frequent petty and not-so-petty thefts.

Collin's goings and comings started to bother me. A succession of teenage thugs began hanging around the property. They didn't wave or say hello. They scurried down the steps, disappearing into the black hole of Collin's lair. Their hair hung in their eyes; they were painfully thin. Their shoulders were hunched, and their hands never left their pockets. ⟿

(Mrs. Arlins *enters, holding a telephone.* Blair *joins her. They put receivers to their ears.*)

MRS. ARLINS: Is this Mrs. Stewart? Mrs. Leonard Stewart? This is Mrs. Arlins.

BLAIR: Yes. I'm sorry. I don't recognize your name.

MRS. ARLINS: I'm Scott's mother.

BLAIR: I'm afraid I don't know anyone named Scott.

MRS. ARLINS: He's a friend of Collin's.

BLAIR: (*uncomfortably*) Well, you see—I don't keep track of Collin's friends. He works for me, but he has his own phone in his quarters. If you'd like the number ...

MRS. ARLINS: (*cutting in*) Mrs. Stewart, I don't want Scott hanging around your house. Collin may be a very nice man, but he's too old to be around the boys. I don't know what Scott and his friends are doing there ... It's just not a good idea, Mrs. Stewart. I would hate to have to put this more strongly to the police.

BLAIR: All right, Mrs. Arlins. I see your point. I'll tell Collin not to invite Scott or those boys here. Thank you for drawing their visits to my attention.

(Blair *hangs up*. Leonard *joins her*. Mrs. Arlins *leaves*.)

LEONARD: What's going on down there? Can YOU figure it out?

BLAIR: It's really not our business.

LEONARD: If he's involved with underage kids, it is our business. This goes on under our roof! We have to take a look inside his apartment. I'll bet he's doing drugs. He'll have the police down our necks.

BLAIR: You're exaggerating. I mean, you and I *drink*. Why shouldn't Collin do what he pleases? His free time should be his own.

LEONARD: What about his influence on those kids? I mean those young hoods Collin has befriended lately.

BLAIR: Come on, Leonard. What's a little marijuana? Those teenagers have cars, so their parents must trust them. And they never come upstairs. I doubt things are missing because of them. I just don't want Scott's mother to get madder than she is.

LEONARD: We have to take a look. The timing is perfect. Collin is in Falls Village.

BLAIR: Do you know how to break locks?

LEONARD: Get me your nail file.

✎ Break it, he did. We opened the door and turned on the light. Every one of Collin's three rooms was overflowing with garbage and empty soda cans. Dirty clothes, empty pizza boxes, crusts of stale bread were piled like mountains of trash you'd find in a garbage dump. Mouse turds spilled from the stale containers like marbles. Gray tee shirts with stained armpits poked out from under chairs. Male sex magazines were strewn on tabletops. In the bathroom were fixtures crusted with scum. There were filthy combs growing hair, paper cups, broken plates, broken china with food stuck on them like pancake makeup.

I thought I was going to vomit. We both took deep breaths and hurried upstairs. We found a box of green leaf bags. I went to the store and bought bottle after bottle of disinfectant, rubber gloves for both of us, then returned. We spent the whole evening cleaning and throwing out.

When we were through, we sat upstairs and asked ourselves why we had never gone downstairs before. Why we hadn't been interested or curious enough to see the underbelly of the man we had been living with all these years. ↩

B L A I R : Collin's such a private person. I wanted to respect that trait. Look where it got us.

L E O N A R D : I feel crapped on. I feel used. I feel he hates us. I'm firing him.

B L A I R : I don't blame you. Still, I feel terrible for him. Our house is always neat. He's responsible for making it that way. Why does he keep it so nice for us and so ugly for himself? I don't understand. I want to help him, not fire him. Ambivalence, huh? I feel I need to ask a shrink why I'm even considering not kicking him out immediately. I mean, why am I sorry for him, at this point? I guess I've *always* been sorry for him.

L E O N A R D : Forget the shrink. I've had it! He's out!!

B L A I R : Well, if for no other reason, I need a shrink to tell me why I've put up with someone like him.

L E O N A R D : You said we needed him.

B L A I R : You thought so, *too*. The pity is … I still do. We can't afford three people to take his place.

L E O N A R D : We'll see. Come on. Let's take this stuff to the dump. (*They exit.*)

⤳ When Collin returned, he was silent for the first day. We didn't say a word, either. All three of us moved around like rats in the same cage. We noted his noting the broken lock to his room. He didn't ask why. He didn't even act as furious as I supposed he would. Honestly, we didn't know what to say. The situation was too grave for me to yell. He was obviously wishing it would all go away. I almost cried, I was so angry at him. Then, I became angry with myself and tried an attitude of just plain disdain. Finally Leonard broke the ice ⤳

LEONARD: (*to* Collin) How could you live like this? How could you do this to us? It's worse than just messy. It's like shitting in your room, in our house.

COLLIN: (*shaking his head, sulking*) Things got out of hand.

LEONARD: Have you anything else to say to us?

COLLIN: (*darkly*) You broke the lock on my door. You touched my things.

LEONARD: Just what do you think you've done to our things? (*no answer*) What were you and your little buddies doing down there? All that's missing is a dead body. And you're the candidate.

COLLIN: (*hangs his head*) You wanna kill me? I don't care. Go ahead. I'm not so crazy about my life, anyway. I didn't mess up on purpose.

LEONARD: Were you taking drugs, Collin? That's how it looks.

COLLIN: I'll admit it.

LEONARD: I told you so, Blair! All those boys, I said they couldn't be trusted. Were you stealing from us?

BLAIR: (*moans*) But they're so young! I thought they were smoking, that's all.

COLLIN: (*glumly, not facing them*) I'm not doing it anymore. I told them to get lost. And we never stole from you. I wouldn't let them. I already told them not to come here anymore. I'm turning over a new leaf, I promise.

LEONARD: (*disgusted*) It's too late to hand out that crap! You're out!

COLLIN: (*miserably*) I don't blame you. I have it coming. But where will I go? That's what I want to know. I can't hold down a regular job. If I don't work here, there's nowhere else for me to go. Mrs. Marlin's dead. I'm just asking you to give me another chance. That's all I'm asking … another chance.

(Collin *looks at them imploringly, then slinks out. They stare at him as he goes.*)

BLAIR: You watch him pack his things. See that he leaves. Take care of severance …

LEONARD: (*horrified*) Not me! YOU do it.

BLAIR: You can't expect *me* to kick out someone who has been around half my life. (*pauses*) Maybe he's too tired at night to clean his place, after he's exhausted from cleaning ours.

LEONARD: (*backing off*) We'll wait and see what he does. (*hopeful*) Maybe he'll go on his own.

(Blair *glares at* Leonard *as he leaves.*)

BLAIR: Fat chance!

◠ Days went by. Collin stayed. He must have thought Leonard's "You're out!" was just a temporary outburst.

Our needs remained the same. There were still flowers to be cut, meals to be cooked, furniture to be refinished. Collin slunk around, meek, docile and manageable. He fixed his door and put on another lock. He knew we'd change our minds. ◠

Entry Twenty

◠ After my father died, Mother continued to live with Anna and Oscar in the same New York apartment where I lived during my youth. Above all, her apartment was fashionable. She favored the monochromatic look. The only color in that sea of gray was the orange of the throw pillows on the ten-foot couch in the living room, which overlooked Fifth Avenue. The East Side, of course. Mother just went to the West Side to catch the ship to Europe.

She, Anna and Oscar went down to Palm Beach late every fall. She was utterly dependent on them. That was part of the problem. The couple cleaned her house, fed her and drove her places. They became her live-in family, literally her lifeline to the world.

On the surface, there was nothing wrong with that. Mother was happy, they seemed happy. The couple's salary had been appropriately raised throughout the years my father was alive. But then, my mother discovered she had a lump in her right breast. She had to be operated upon. The operation seemed, at first, to be successful, but it wasn't. Shortly after my mother's surgery, Anna demanded an outrageous raise. Only a few weeks later, she asked for another. When the cancer had metastasized to the bone, Mother needed constant attention. Even with the couple, we were forced to hire nurses round-the-clock.

One day, when I was visiting, Anna came marching down the hall. Leonard, as it happened, was there in New York, with me. ↩

(Anna *and* Leonard *enter from different directions.*)

ANNA: I'm glad you come, Mister Stewart. I have much important to say. I want that black nurse out of here! Who does she think she is, telling me what to feed Missus Neville, when I've been taking care of her all these years? Your mother can't eat that mush. And the black one wants me to feed *her*, as well. Of course, I must cook for my husband. That's three different dinners every night.

BLAIR: Anna, Mother's diet has changed. Besides, the doctor spoke to the nurse. She knows what she's doing. And please be quiet about her race.

ANNA: (*hands on hips*) I don't serve blacks!

LEONARD: Now wait a minute! I didn't know Italians held racist beliefs.

BLAIR: (*trying to placate her*) Anna, we really have a good group of nurses this time. Don't spoil it. They are good to Mother, and she likes them. Be civil, all right?

ANNA: (*haughtily*) If the black nurse stays, I want more money.

LEONARD: I don't believe this!

ANNA: If I have to put up with her insolence, I want more money.

LEONARD: (*ironically*) Well, Blair. You have power of attorney. What do you say to THAT request? This would be the third raise in eight months.

BLAIR: Anna, you've made this decision easy for me. You're fired.

ANNA: What did you say?

BLAIR: (*carefully*) In plain English, YOU! ARE! FIRED!

ANNA: (*furious*) You can't *do* that! I'll speak to your mother about this! I'll show you! Right now, I'm going into her bedroom and tell the signora that she has cancer. I'm going to tell her that she is dying, that her daughter is going against her wishes. I'll tell her you are trying to get her money. If this kills her, that's *your* fault!

LEONARD: (*incredulous*) You would do that? You would do that kind of damage? You wouldn't dare, if Joe Neville were alive.

ANNA: Things are not the way they were. No one pushes us around. Thirty years my husband and I've been here. We, not you! We run this house!

(*She makes a rush for the back corridor, and* Leonard *grabs her.*)

L E O N A R D : (*holding her tight as she struggles*) You WORKED here! You ran nothing! Now we want you out!

A N N A : Let me go, Fascist!

O S C A R : (*enters room, stands at door*) She will say nothing. We will leave within the hour. Come, Anna, no more. Let her go, Signor.

(Anna *lowers her head and exits in silence.*)

⮌ Mother had heard the commotion from her room. She called me in to ask what was happening. I told her the couple had to go, that it was an emergency back home, and they were too upset to face her. They sent her their love, said how miserable they were to be leaving her.

As it worked out, Mother died peacefully in the middle of the night, not knowing Anna's perfidy. I was glad about that.

Living with them, I thought, was like having vipers in the house.

Collin was never vicious. After Mother's funeral, he surprised me as I was sitting in the library looking out the window, with some tea and a lovely vase of yellow crocuses. He said, quietly, "These are like the ones I gave you the first day we met. I wanted you to have them, in remembrance of your mother. She meant a lot to me, too. Every time I eat corn on the cob, I think of her."

I burst out laughing, then into tears, and realized why it

would be impossible for me to give Collin up. I had lost both my parents. I couldn't face another abandonment.

Neither Scott Arlins nor the other boys ever visited Collin again; he had seemed healthier and had been in a better frame of mind for a long time. No talk of suicide, no spaced-out staring. We were getting the Warwick Way house ready to sell. There were workmen everywhere. We bought a Tudor-style place near a private club in Greenwich, only forty-five minutes from Manhattan. No more basement apartments for us or Collin. We'd bring him upstairs where we could keep our eye on him. Collin would be all right, if we just exercised a little oversight.

We were moving into a better neighborhood, close to the mainstream of restaurants and shops. Just what I wanted. Months went by. We moved and Collin unpacked and, in the winter, we went to our house in the Florida Keys, in Marathon.

The kids graduated from college, first Mark, the next year, Kay. They went happily off to their own pursuits.

On long winter weekends, Leonard and I shuttled back and forth between Greenwich and the Keys. Collin drove ahead with the dogs, Ophelia and the youngster, Puck, to get the place ready. He stayed down there all winter to keep it open for us, the children and our friends. There was so much for Collin to do that no one had time to worry about drugs or broken locks or stolen money. ⤺

Entry Twenty-One

⌒ Collin didn't look right, the last winter we were together in the Keys. Although he was dragging slightly, recovering from the flu, nothing would stop him from pruning the palm trees. He loved working outside there, just as he loved the view of Bonefish Harbor from our second-floor porch. But he never stopped complaining that Marathon was so far from Key West, where he loved to go to watch the dancing at the Strand. Forty-five minutes away didn't seem so far to me, not after almost ten years in Falls Village.

Yet all wasn't well. Collin developed terrible bronchitis. He claimed he had it just before he left for the South, and then, when he got down there, even the warm weather didn't help.

Still, he puffed on his pipe, as he weeded around the oleander and the bougainvillea. He also smoked a pack of cigarettes a day. After the children were born, Leonard and I had given up smoking. We hated the smell. I begged Collin not to smoke in the house, but he proceeded to do so. As usual, we carped, then let him do as he pleased.

Collin was still too sick to come north when we flew back in Leonard's plane to Greenwich in March. We let him stay, hoping his bronchitis would clear up. He wrote he was getting the Florida house shipshape and that he had a new friend, Emory. No last name.

We agreed he should stay in Marathon until the end of April. Then we insisted he come home. Finally, he said he was on his way.

We waited for days, expecting Collin. To our amazement he arrived, looking hunched and unwell, late one afternoon with Emory in tow, unannounced and unexpected. Emory turned out to be older than the basement crowd had been, better-looking, but shifty-eyed and ill at ease, just the same. He was tall and attractive with blond, lank hair and a handsome face. His skin was very white for someone who had just come from the Keys, his eyes were blue, weak and watery. He didn't hold my gaze for very long. He had a look of the transient about him. It was obvious he didn't know what to make of our world up here on a mini-estate in the sophisticated town of Greenwich, as low-key as Leonard and I were in our own home.

I can understand our place putting Emory off. The first day we moved, I lost the address, the number of the house, and dropped into the main post office to ask the postmaster. He chuckled. "Mrs. Stewart," he said. "If you live on Silver Spruce Lane you don't need to know the number." ⌇

(*It's a gray day.* Collin *gets out of the car slowly. He looks list-less.* Blair *joins him.*)

B L A I R : Damn it, you should have told me you were bring-ing Emory. I'm sorry, Collin. If you're going to ask if he can stay ... there's no room. Why didn't you speak to us in ad-vance?

C O L L I N : (*doesn't look her in the face*) My bronchitis is bad. I don't seem to be able to shake it. Emory helped me drive. Besides, he'll help me get the place ready for summer.

B L A I R : You only have one bed in your room. Where do you propose he sleep?

(Collin *doesn't answer.*)

B L A I R : (*shrugs*) So, it's out of the closet with a vengeance. Well, I don't care. I just don't like the idea of a stranger in your room—in my house. Besides, he doesn't look me in the eye. I don't know anything about him.

C O L L I N : He's all right. Don't worry. He says he likes you.

B L A I R : What do I care if he likes me?

C O L L I N : Don't get excited. He hasn't any money. It's just for a week or so, until I help him find a job. Then he'll leave.

B L A I R : Wait a minute. He has no money? No way to earn a living?

C O L L I N : Your garden is full of leaves. A week's work and he's out of here. Really, Lady ... I need the help. It's too much for me these days.

(*Before she can respond,* Collin *exits.*)

It was late in the day, and Collin was shivering. I felt concerned that the flu hadn't left him, so I thought I'd wait to deal with Emory. I knew Collin was manipulating me, but he looked positively awful. As I walked up the stairs to my room and looked up to the third floor, it suddenly occurred to me that Collin and Emory would be having sex up there. I wasn't as liberal when my imagination took hold, I'm afraid. Even my daughter's bisexuality was giving me trouble.

(Leonard *joins her on the stairs.*)

LEONARD: (*whispers*) What's the matter? Come into our room and close the door. (*They enter the bedroom.*) Now, tell me the problem.

BLAIR: Nothing, I suppose. I just realized this is the first time Collin has blatantly had a man in his bed in our house. I don't get it, Leonard. We suspected he was gay, but he's hidden it all these years. Now, sex right over our heads ... those two guys? I hate that Emory.

LEONARD: I don't like him, either. Tell him to get out in the morning. (*stands*) I'm going down to the basement to check the pressure on the hot water tank. (*exits*)

BLAIR: (stunned) Me tell him? Damn! (*calls down the stairs*) You come back here, Leonard. (*no answer*)

 Leonard was gone again by morning. He had a big meeting with a new industrial tenant. Once again, he was leaving the firing line.

There was gardening, and dishes and clothes to be washed. I became distracted. Collin cooked, and Emory stayed in their room. I put him out of my mind, went to bed early, read a few scripts, and slept.

Several days went by. On the fourth day, I finally got around to asking Collin to send Emory away. ⌒

(Collin *enters and kneels before the flower garden.* Blair *stands next to him.*)

BLAIR: Why are you doing this to me, Collin? Is Emory leaving at the end of the week? I want him gone.

COLLIN: He's been no harm. This morning he helped me break ground for the vegetable garden. We put in a bed of lettuce and squash. Just wait until he can get a little cash, so he can rent an apartment.

BLAIR: He's not my problem! Stop pushing me! (*pause*) Don't look so downcast. He'll manage. He managed before you came along. (*pauses again*) Tell him thanks for the garden, will you?

COLLIN: (*smiles*) I will. In a day or so, I promise ...

(Collin *salutes timidly and goes over to the vegetable garden.* Emory *enters.* Collin *tenderly pokes* Emory *in the arm as they dig and whisper together.* Collin *laughs at everything* Emory *says. He is obviously enamored.* Blair *watches.*)

⌒ I'll be damned. Collin was in love. I had the feeling this was Collin's first real love affair. We—most of us—take it for granted that love affairs are inevitable, or a possibility, at least. Not so Collin. I had been spoiled. For better or worse, I had had love all my life. Suddenly, I saw how much this meant to him. It made me feel sad and permissive. I let things ride. I decided to let Emory stay.

Leonard had to spend the next few nights in New York, he said. He telephoned and said he'd bring home a painting I had admired on Madison Avenue. He sent his kisses. I hoped he'd changed. I didn't want to worry about his tail-hunting habits anymore.

Late one night, Leonard called me. I was in bed when the phone rang. All the gardening had exhausted Collin and Emory; they had retired early to the room above mine. It was raining outside. My reading light was on, but I wasn't having much success concentrating on my play. ✎

LEONARD: (*holding phone*) How're you doing? What's with Collin and Emory?

BLAIR: I think Collin's in love for the first time. How can I take this away from him? I'm a coward, too. Just like you. Still, I don't like having them upstairs. I keep wondering what they're doing up there. It's so quiet. Too quiet. And Emory hasn't found a job. That annoys me. He's just simply *there!* And I suspect they're drinking.

LEONARD: For cryin' out loud, you must be nuts. It's our house! You don't have to put up with this. Get rid of him! Oh, never mind. I'll be home in a day or two. I'll tell him to leave.

BLAIR: (*laughs*) Sure. Besides, it won't do much good. Collin's will is stronger than both of ours put together. He'll find a way to prolong Emory's stay. (*looks up at the ceiling*) Collin gets so tired. I wonder if he's contemplating going off with Emory? What do you think?

LEONARD: I think we'd better learn to do without Collin. I told you, I think he's ambivalent about wanting to stay, anyway. Sleep well. I'll call you in the morning.

(Blair *hangs up, but remains in bed. She starts to doze. Out of the blue, there is a loud noise upstairs as something bangs against a wall.*)

BLAIR: (*sits up, alarmed*) Dear God, what's that?

(*A scuffle and a loud crash—then a moan.* Emory *shouts,* "Get her! Get her!")

(*whispers, frightened*) Oh, my God! Leonard's away. I'm all alone here. What does Emory mean, "Get her, get her"? (*dreadful pause*) Does he mean go fetch her or go *hurt* her? Maybe Emory is furious, or hates me. How can Collin expose me to trouble like this?

(Blair *hears shouts. The cry* "Fight!" *rings out. It is* Emory *again.*)

BLAIR: (*jumps up*) I can't stand this! Those sounds. In a moment I expect the door to be smashed open, and Emory to hurtle down the stairs. Call the police? No! What if he picks up the extension and hears me? Besides, they won't get here in time.

EMORY'S VOICE: (*in despair*) What's a' matter? Hit me!

Hit me! Damn it, I tell you, hit me!

BLAIR: He's obviously drunk. And what is he capable of doing? I hear Collin trying to soothe him.

EMORY'S VOICE: I hurt you. I know I did. Hit me! Hit me! HIT ME!

COLLIN'S VOICE: Calm down, it's all right. I don't want *her* to hear you.

↩ I pulled on my clothes and crept down the stairs. Then I went outside to my car, crawled inside in the dark, and locked the doors. ↩

BLAIR: (*a gasp of relief*) Safe! (*with more confidence*) Thank God, I don't have to summon the police. They would probably arrive with sirens blaring. Leonard is big on reputation. It would be a great relief to him if I didn't lose my head and scream, or didn't wake the neighbors. A great relief that our reputation in town wouldn't be destroyed. "My dear, there are brawls in the Stewart household, ugly scenes in the middle of the night." The neighbors might think it was *Leonard and I.* I'd better pull the car down to the end of the block. Keep my lights off. Thank heaven for car phones. (*picks up receiver and pushes buttons*)

(Collin *and* Emory *are still upstairs.* Emory *crouches, his head in his hands. Phone rings.* Collin *picks up the receiver.*)

COLLIN: Hello?

BLAIR: Are you crazy, or what? Listen, I'm really angry at

you, Collin! I told you to make him leave. Now it's come to this. I want him out now! (*still on the phone*) I was on my way to a motel without a suitcase. Let *him* go to a motel. I'm not fleeing my own house.

COLLIN: (*Grasping his side, he makes an effort to speak normally.*) He hasn't any money.

BLAIR: You sound funny. Are you in pain?

COLLIN: I'm okay. Don't worry. Emory's fine now.

BLAIR: (*cautiously*) What's that noise?

COLLIN: He's crying. He's sorry. He's apologizing all over the place. (*He bends down, caressing* Emory, *trying to soothe him.*)

BLAIR: (*gritting her teeth*) He's hurt you. You just won't admit it. *You* might be a masochist, but I'm not. You're trying to manipulate me again. I won't have it.

COLLIN: (*breathing hard, hesitates*) I'll get him out. I said I would and I will.

BLAIR: He's to leave! He should take all his stuff. I don't want him to have an excuse to come back, Collin. He beat you? You'd let him stay? You must be sick. Collin, do you hear me? Don't you understand? He's a violent drinker, who would beat up the one man who gave him sanctuary. If you're too stupid to be afraid of him, let me tell you, I'm *not*.

COLLIN: (*pleasantly*) All right.

BLAIR: *When?*

COLLIN: First thing in the morning.

BLAIR: (*takes a deep breath*) I'm waiting here for you *now!*

Drive the station wagon by me so I see you take him. Then I'll
go back in. You drop him off somewhere and then come home.

COLLIN: All right. (*He hangs up, but stays in place.*)

BLAIR: (*Hangs up. Waits. Looks at her watch.* Collin *is
crouching over* Emory, *holding him, rocking him, saying, "It's all
right. There, there. You'll be all right."*) Twenty minutes have
gone by! (*picks up and dials again, hisses angrily*) Collin!

COLLIN: (*picks up receiver again*) Yes?

BLAIR: Where the hell are you, damn it? Why haven't you
left? I'm waiting at the end of the drive for you to pass. It's almost midnight. I want to come home.

COLLIN: (*miserably*) He'll go in the morning. Later this
morning. I promise. Leave me alone.

BLAIR: Now. Damn it. *Now!* Are you deaf? You want me to
call the police to throw you both out? I swear I'll call them,
Collin. I swear I will. You're taking advantage of me because
Leonard is away.

COLLIN: (*after awhile*) Lady, can you lend me some
money? He hasn't funds to stay anywhere.

BLAIR: Why should I pay him anything?

COLLIN: If you don't, he can't leave. Where can he sleep?
On Greenwich Avenue? I'll pay you back out of my salary.

BLAIR: You'll never see that money again. Neither will I.
How much?

COLLIN: (*sighing*) Enough for the motel and a ticket back
down south.

BLAIR: Oh, Christ! A ticket too? You're lucky I went to the

bank this morning.

COLLIN: I'll pay you back.

BLAIR: You're damn right, you *will!* Now get down here.

(*They both hang up.* Collin *and* Emory *stand not far from* Blair. Emory *has a nylon over-the-shoulder bag and is crying.* Collin *comes over to her. Silently she hands him the money.*)

BLAIR: I don't want to talk to him. Keep him away from me.

EMORY: (*takes a step toward her, hand outstretched*) Please, please forgive me, Mrs. Stewart. You've been good to me. I appreciate it. I didn't mean anything bad.

BLAIR: You hurt Collin, and you frightened me, Emory. You were violent. I have nothing against you, I'm just afraid to have you in my house.

(Blair *watches as they go off.*)

↩ I was damned sorry for Emory, angry at Collin and at myself for being taken in. But Collin looked so bad that I was pretty sure his ribs were broken, and I couldn't put up with abuse. You could tell he hurt. He was as white as a ghost and hunched over. In the morning, I insisted he go to the hospital and have himself checked. ↪

Entry Twenty-Two

⌒ The day after Emory left, Collin went into the hospital for observation. Dr. Walters examined him. Three days later, Leonard and I were sitting on the porch, arguing. We were alone in the house, but Leonard was still whispering. They told Leonard first. As if I wouldn't have had to find out, sooner or later. I was shocked, but not totally surprised.

LEONARD: Don't you dare tell any one!

BLAIR: (*sits next to him*) What difference does it make? There is no way people aren't going to find out.

LEONARD: Don't you know there's a stigma attached to the very word? My God, you tell your friends, it'll be all over Stamford and Greenwich like wildfire. They'll say, "Maybe we'd better not go to their house." Our beautiful house tainted for good. All the money we spent. No one will visit.

BLAIR: Damn your precious house! People know better than that, Leonard. (*thoughtfully*) It's so funny. You brought me to Falls Village and didn't understand how I felt, when nobody wanted to visit me. Now you're worried nobody will come and visit us in Greenwich and all because of poor Collin. How do you reconcile your attitudes, then and now?

LEONARD: This is an entirely different situation. This time the prejudice won't disappear.

∽ Leonard might have been partially right, but I thought his attitude so trivial, even cruel, in light of what was going to happen to Collin. Collin would be fifty that October. He was a Scorpio. Scorpios were supposed to be master criminals or detectives. For fifty years Collin was master of nothing, not even his own sex life. His vulnerability had been his destruction.

The other night I saw a Rock Hudson movie on television and thought to myself, now that the whole world knows he had AIDS, had died of it, Rock Hudson would no longer be the gorgeous hunk a woman dreamed about, a symbol of the men she loved. It seemed to me his memory was sullied. Pictures of that poor, ravaged face before he died superimposed themselves over Collin's, in my mind. I realized that every time I saw a Rock Hudson film, thoughts of *that* disease would be conjured up. A man died of AIDS, and his memory was contaminated. I didn't want that to happen to Collin … My God, how could I tell him we knew? He cared so terribly what people thought. ∽

LEONARD: I don't know what you plan to do, but don't, Blair! I mean it! Don't breathe a word of this!

BLAIR: Leonard, be logical. People read the papers. Everyone knows you have to have intercourse or use a dirty needle or get a transfusion or something. People won't feel in jeopardy if they come to our house. Our friends are too intelligent for that.

LEONARD: You're kidding yourself. No one has an open mind when their life is threatened. Oh, I believe people *want* to be liberal. But I've heard them say, "What if the virus becomes airborne?" What if it's out there, floating around, or like germs trapped in fabric on a couch, or chair … in the home where the patient lives? What if it's there for keeps, no matter what experts the newspapers quote? Our friends might say, for safety's sake, "Better not go to the Stewarts', after all." Just in case, is what they'll say! "And what were the Stewarts doing with a man like that around so long?" they might ask. "Maybe one of them is infected, too. He cooked their food."

It's true, Blair. People are fine as long as it doesn't affect their lives or their wallets. Don't be stupid. It's our future in this town that can be affected. Keep your mouth shut, all right, Darling? (*She looks reluctant.*) This lovely house … some people might pronounce it off-limits, and you don't want that, do you?

BLAIR: I can't believe you're saying this. People would think *that,* just because our employee might have AIDS?

LEONARD: Yes, just because he *does.* Believe me! They'll say, "Maybe we'd better not go there … at least for a time."

BLAIR: I don't believe you.

LEONARD: And I don't want you to find out I'm right.

BLAIR: He's so angry, Leonard. He called a nurse in the hospital a cunt. He's wild with rage. He makes me feel as if I'm to blame, and I know it's only because he's so scared.

LEONARD: God, Blair. This is a death sentence. It makes me realize what a short time we all have.

BLAIR: I know.

LEONARD: (*embraces her*) You're my whole life, Blair. I hope you realize that. It's time we do something together again.

BLAIR: (*puts her head on his shoulder*) We can try.

LEONARD: Right now, Collin's future has to be considered. We'll have to find a place for him. (Leonard *kisses* Blair *and leaves.*)

✍ Later that night, the children returned my calls. I told them our bad news, told Mark what his father had said. Mark said, "Dad's right. You shouldn't let Collin stay. You have no idea what you're letting yourself in for, Mom. You don't owe Collin anything more."

Kay was more charitable. She had visited AIDS patients in several group homes. She worked part-time as a trainer, an exercise therapist, and was better informed than her brother. Due to the time difference from California, her call came several hours after his. ✍

BLAIR: (*holding phone receiver*) Kay, your father's worried about AIDS in our home, now that Collin has it. What do you think?

KAY: (*with receiver*) Mom, don't worry about catching it. Not unless you're using needles, or something.

BLAIR: Of course not! (*pauses, speaks despairingly*) All these years, I've been so blind about what was going on under my own roof. Not just Collin, but Leonard too. And you children. How could I have been so gullible?

KAY: Don't torture yourself, Mom. You can't change people, especially us. You couldn't stop Collin from catching AIDS, from living, doing what he does. What does it matter, now?

✍ Trying to figure if there was such a thing as right or wrong, I perceived certain truths from the patterns of Collin's behavior. Did I blame Collin for destroying himself? Blame, as I said before, is something I don't like to deal with, in myself or in anyone else. In a way, he did commit suicide after all.

Stress and blame always ran rampant in the Stewart household and, whenever there was too much of it, I rationalized, auditioned, performed on stage, worked in my garden, wrote in my journal and tried to think beautiful thoughts. Mother raised me to ignore the ugly. The whole world was like a fine dining table, where nothing unpleasant was allowed to be discussed. It was my duty to see no evil. Oh, Mother, now I have to grow up without you! You kept me a little girl too long.

Collin destroyed himself right in our own home. This was the first time I've mentioned that to anyone. It was done with sex or drugs, and we had known about both. It took me months to be able to confront the issue.

I never fully faced the fact that, for most of the time he lived with us, Collin was hooked on drugs. He took them furtively, the way some people drink. I now realized he got high with his teenage friends in order to keep up with them, to do what they did so they would like him. He was always apart, as separate as the day he met me coming along that country road, as separate and lonely as I was. And since there was no way to stop it, the loneliness burrowed into the soft flesh of his heart and stayed, glued like the ticks on my dogs. That loneliness destroyed his peace of mind, but Collin destroyed himself.

I hated the thought! Destroying yourself over anything was such a waste! I had the resources to change my life: I, at least, had mental health, financial security, and a family to fall back on. Collin had none. And why didn't his friends stop him? *What* friends? His family? His sister moved away and his brother was an alcoholic. Drinking and smoking yourself into oblivion was a common enough pastime up in those pastoral fields of Litchfield County, as well as in New York City, the Florida Keys and Greenwich itself. As far as dulling boredom and that useless feeling that comes with self-doubt, Collin was no different from his brother or from much of the human race.

Let me read from my journal:

"Collin, I wonder where you are now and if you can ever understand how I am feeling. Love is at issue here. Love you, gawky, old Collin. If only you could hear that, you'd snort with laughter. Well, one can love all sorts, you know. Even you. You never knew how I needed you, did you? Nor did I. I never understood that in my fashion I actually loved you. You were so worried I'd write about you one day. You made me swear I'd leave you out of everything I ever wrote. Well, I swore to it, and even as I made that silly promise, I knew I was lying. I knew you'd end up, at the very least, in the pages of this journal. How could I *not* include you?

"You are a juicy morsel, Collin. And I believe that what happened between you and Leonard and me mattered. Love is always what makes the difference. All kinds of love: odd love, young love, love that grows and warps over the years like your strange caring for me. And in the case of our family's love for you … it was a love we never even knew was there. I think about you so often, Collin. You really were my best friend. I wish I had tried harder to be yours."

So, at best, this is the story of a marriage: Leonard's, mine and Collin's. A household of three adults, two children, two dogs who came later and a cat named Mitzu, who got eaten. It's a dangerous world out there.

Now I would say we were a *"ménage à sept. "* All cloistered in our Tudor house, seemingly safe and warm. Straight out of an old English print. Seven of us in one house, including the children and animals. Animals were big in our family. White dogs snuggled by our hearth and in our beds. Collin adored the dogs. When I didn't, he slept with them. God, I'll bet he misses them now. ⌒

Entry Twenty-Three

⌒ With Leonard on business in California and Collin in the hospital, I was alone in my house for the first time in twenty years. I felt shocked and horrified. Just to think of Collin fatally ill, creating scenes in his semiprivate room with the nurses and doctors.

Our relationship had been as complicated as my marriage. But what could I have done all those years? Collin simply was not fireable. Oh, I knew I had let it get this way. I just let him run the thousand errands, do the thousand tasks that made life so much easier for me. And because I let him, agreed to carry the heavy burden of his ineptitude, his low-life friends, his probable drug habit, his refusal to deal with his own affairs, I was now *stuck* with him.

Bill, our decorator friend, telephoned with more news. Shakespeare said it for us all. Trouble comes not in single spies, but in battalions. ⌒

(Bill *enters. He looks as if his world has collapsed. He is un-shaven, his eyes dark with misery.*)

BILL: (*speaks to* Blair, *his voice breaking*) I was sorry I couldn't be more help to you, Blair, when you called about Collin. But you see, I can't sympathize when my own darling boy is dying. John didn't take drugs. Once, he stepped out. *Once!* Otherwise, we've been so happy. You see, I'm the elder. I always thought I'd go first. I worried how he'd fare without me. (*begins to cry*) Now it's me who's going to be left alone. I can't stand it. I want to die, too, Blair. John's as loyal in this marriage as any human being could be. He is good to my family, to me ... improbably good! I can't see how I can survive this. (*pauses, speaks bitterly*) He's nothing like Collin. Living that low life! And the worst of it is ... the world will mass Collin and John together in the same set of statistics, declare that they're the same. Well, they're not! Oh, God, they're not. One was a gentleman. The other, a poor sad whore. (*exits*)

⬦ I didn't believe Collin was a whore, but I wasn't going to argue. The boys had had so much. They had something special for so many years, while Collin remained alone—except for us. I can't even count Emory. There was so little I could say. Nothing I could do to comfort Bill. I went to my desk and sat down, trying to cheer myself by turning on the radio. A nostalgic melody came on. One of the old romantic songs Collin loved. I wondered if he was listening in the hospital.

Collin was crazy for those songs from the fifties. His room

was always filled with love songs. He immortalized the decade when he was a boy. He made it obvious that those days of his youth were worth remembering. It's as if he stopped dreaming at fifteen. No deep, long-standing love came to him as it did to us, as it did to Bill and John. No one ever really loved him like that. Even our own feelings for him were stained by confusion and role-playing.

Collin came home from the hospital with his ribs bandaged, still complaining about bronchitis. I said nothing to him, knowing he had AIDS, knowing he was hiding it. As Leonard insisted, I avoided the subject, except for the children, to everyone but Bill. I had a hell of a time pretending ignorance, tending to Collin, feeding him, afraid he was contagious … then ashamed.

Weeks went by. It was all Leonard and I talked about those days—Collin having AIDS. We didn't know how to handle him. I didn't know what to say to him half the time. Collin was upstairs getting thinner, ignoring his illness.

I felt as if I were rolling a huge stone up a muddy hill. Then I joined a support group for friends and relatives whose loved ones had contracted AIDS. I learned Collin was in a state of denial. The very sound of his whistling as he went about his daily tasks of watering plants and vacuuming carpets was driving me to distraction.

Collin's mental and physical well-being, I realized, should be my immediate concern. Understand, he was supposed to be going for treatment to Dr. Walters. Well, he wasn't. Collin was furious at the doctor. For a while, he went to the hospital for inhalation therapy. Then he stopped and refused everything else. Dr. Walters told us he never wanted to handle him again. I didn't blame him. When Collin felt threatened, he acted as if everyone were his enemy. If he got sick again, where could we send him?

I knew he should be in a support group, but I didn't know how to broach the subject. Some days he managed for himself, but when the pain was severe, I had to climb two flights of stairs to our top floor and bring him his meals.

The doctor told Leonard that Collin would cut his life in half if he didn't get treatment. But what could I do, when he just went about as if he were going to live forever? I thought he believed they had diagnosed the wrong man.

That was when I went to the support group. I took my cousin Joanie with me. That was a mistake, let me tell you. I never knew how much she disliked Collin, or that she was homophobic. ⪜

(*The support group sits around the table. They wait for* Blair *and* Joanie *to be seated: the* Young Woman, Eleanor, Jerry *and* Dr. Sherman.)

DR. SHERMAN: Tell him! Speak right out, kindly but firmly. The big problem is that Collin doesn't admit to being gay, and so it's hard to suggest he go to the Gay Men's Health Crisis Group for support. He might hate me for suggesting that, if he won't say he's gay. Too, drugs might be the way he contracted the disease.

ELEANOR: It's *his* disease. This isn't your burden. Try to be a little more removed from the panic of the situation, Blair. Remaining his friend is really all you can be expected to do.

DR. SHERMAN: You can't live another person's life for him. Blair, you and your husband keeping him on salary and paying for his medical insurance is the greatest gift you can give him.

BLAIR: Leonard still refuses to tell our friends about Collin. Now I'm mad at Leonard. At least Collin has Joanie's support and mine. He'll need friends more than ever now.

YOUNG WOMAN: Your husband is absolutely right. My husband has it. I didn't tell anyone, except good friends.

ELEANOR: I have a daughter who got AIDS from her husband, who is drug-addicted. She left him. She's twenty-three. I worked all my life. Now I live with my daughter. We don't have the money to pay for AZT treatments. Neither of us has insurance. If I bring my daughter to the hospital, they won't treat her unless we can pay on the spot.

DR. SHERMAN: My AIDS patients in the Greenwich area have been increasing in number. In the office where I practice, we don't mention the disease.

JERRY: (*interrupting*) My lover has AIDS. I have AIDS-related complex. My advice to you, Eleanor, is bluff it. Get your daughter into the hospital, no matter what.

YOUNG WOMAN: We've been encouraged to live a freer sexual life since the sixties. Now some right-wingers are saying that AIDS is God's punishment for being immoral or promiscuous.

BLAIR: People's abilities to sympathize are so different. But Collin's so alone. Take you, Joanie. How do you feel about letting people like Collin into your life?

JOANIE: (*stands*) You are very nice people ... and I ... well ... It's hard for me to speak. In fact, I resent being asked. (*upset—getting defensive, angry*) I ... I don't mean to be hardhearted or anything. I'm charity-minded. I work at the Hammerville Nursing Home two days a week. Old age ... now *there's* a tragedy I can identify with. No, I have entirely too much to do to help Collin. (*prepares to leave*) I realize there are awful illnesses everywhere you look, and I *do* sympathize. Your stories are very sad, but AIDS is not a very respectable cause to be fighting for. How can you expect people to identify with dirty needles? Or homosexuality? I'm sorry, Jerry, but you chose that lifestyle. You have to deal with the result.

Besides, everyone understands that AIDS will die out. It'll be gone soon. You'll see.

BLAIR: (*furious*) I'm appalled. You're supposed to be sophisticated. What on earth is a nonrespectable disease, anyway? How can you be so indifferent in front of these people, who have to cope every day? And what does "die out" mean? Diseases don't die out! They're here to stay until someone finds a cure.

JOANIE: Slow down or be cured, that's what I meant. It'll probably just fade away after those who have it are ... ah ... gone.

DR. SHERMAN: Bull! It's hitting the heterosexual community now.

BLAIR: (*distressed*) I'm horrified to hear you talk this way, Joanie. So prejudiced ... so unfeeling ... I thought you would be Collin's friend. You've known him long enough. He makes special dishes for you, when you come over.

JOANIE: (*interrupting*) Blair, Dear. I can't help it if I feel the way that young woman described ... that AIDS is God telling us something. That's how I feel. I can't pretend otherwise.

BLAIR: Oh, please. Not the old retribution crap! You were so kind when Mother died. I thought ...

JOANIE: I loved your mother. She was my *aunt.* Really, I only spoke my mind. I'm sorry I let you talk me into coming here. This is just not my concern. Oh, I feel for you people, but I never really liked Collin. I always thought he was irresponsible with his life ... just like his teenage drop-in buddies, but older. He did it to himself. Let himself go, was casual with the way he lived. I'm sorry, Blair, but I told you to fire him years ago. Well, that's how I still feel. Good luck, all the rest of you. (*She grabs her purse and hurries out.*)

BLAIR: (*speaks to group*) I'm sorry ... I shouldn't have put her on the spot.

DR. SHERMAN: Don't you think we're used to it? Don't

worry. Shall we move on? There's an interesting theory about the similarity between syphilis and the AIDS virus. Syphilis also lays dormant for many years and causes a distortion of the immune system. It used to be considered a punishment for immoral behavior, even though innocent people were affected, too.

JERRY: (*excited*) In the play *Ghosts* by Ibsen? I think the feelings Oswald had, the depression and guilt because he thought he was tainted, might be similar to the way an AIDS patient feels. It's as if in every age, every decade, some disease is discovered that distorts the immune system. And it is always given a new horrible name and a new set of victims, who are labeled "untouchables." (*calmer*) Oh, I feel well now. Optimistic about my lover, about his health, about my own. Each time his fever goes away, I have hope that tomorrow will be a good day. And when things get bad? Well, who knows if they'll find a cure tomorrow? Any day now. Whatever happens, I plan to help others as long as I can. That's what this support group is all about, isn't it?

YOUNG WOMAN: The weeks seem so long! I know I can't wait for these meetings. I have no one else to talk to. As you see … you can't talk to anyone outside. They don't understand.

BLAIR: When Mother was diagnosed with cancer, at least she was treated with a sympathy you obviously are not getting.

ELEANOR: My daughter and I—we live in one room at the top of my old house. My stepchildren live downstairs with their little kids. I took them in to help financially. Now, they won't let my daughter come into their apartment. They condemn her for marrying at fifteen, especially for marrying a man who was into drugs, and I can't afford to ask them to move. My daughter is so depressed, she'll only hang out with her ex-husband's druggie crowd. She says *they* accept her.

JERRY: Can't you move your daughter away?

ELEANOR: I work, but I don't have the money. How on earth can we afford to move? Dr. Sherman, can you suggest where I can take her? Can I bring her to you in Greenwich?

DR. SHERMAN: By all means, Eleanor. You'll have to wait, though, until I find another office. My associates have asked me to move out.

ELEANOR: That's horrible.

DR. SHERMAN: It's also understandable. I have so many AIDS patients, they're just worried we're going to lose our other patients. Too specialized, one of my aged colleagues suggested. Such is human nature, my friends. With the old guard, that is. Don't worry, the thinking will change.

BLAIR: In the meantime … what am I to do about Collin?

DR. SHERMAN: Just understand the stages. Denial, anger, depression, acceptance. You must tell him everything you know, Blair. He has to be informed.

(*The support group leaves.*)

↬ So finally, I told him. I sat him down on a beautiful, sunny summer afternoon, stopped him as he went whistling out the door on his way to water the roses in our garden. It was certainly *our* garden. He loved it as much as I did. ⌐

(Collin *picks up the hose. He is whistling. The light is on him.* Blair *stands and slowly walks toward him.*)

⌐ Inside, my heart fluttered. I had a sick feeling in my stomach, and my ears buzzed the way they do when you can't believe anything happening around you is real. I had improvised this conversation a hundred times. I had pictured myself gently putting my hand on his shoulder, imparting the bad news in a soft, steady voice. Even so, with all the rehearsing, I was in a cold sweat. ⌐

BLAIR: (*She stands behind* Collin, *speaks casually, softly.*) Stop a minute, Collin. Please sit down. (*They sit.* Blair *takes a deep breath.*) Collin, I know you tested positive for AIDS and I wish you'd stop trying to keep it a secret from me, because I love you. I'm on your side. I'm your friend, I'll always be your friend and I want to help. Leonard and I want nothing but the best for you. I want you to believe that!

COLLIN: (*exploding*) That doctor! He told you. That dirty bastard Walters!! God damn him! I'm going to sue that son of a bitch! He had no right to talk about me behind my back.

BLAIR: Walters *had* to tell us! But Collin, we didn't need him to tell us. We were terrified from your appearance that you were gravely ill. At least, we were pretty sure. We wanted to help you, Collin. And that's why we asked the hospital to test you.

COLLIN: (*releasing tension*) Well, I still say he had a terrible nerve. I could sue him for this … but never mind. You're the only one who really cares about me. I'll do whatever you like. You tell me what to do, and I'll do it. By the way, your dry cleaning should be ready. I'll pick it up. What shall we have for dinner? I thought I'd cook some broiled chicken and make some chocolate pudding …

(Collin *goes off*. Blair *shakes her head slowly*.)

 Entry Twenty-Four

↪ What had I been afraid of? Collin hardly reacted at all. Still ignored what he didn't like. Things didn't change. He agreed to be cooperative, but days went by, and he didn't do anything but continue to deny his illness, and rail against Dr. Walters.

There wasn't a minute when I wasn't thinking it all out for him. He wouldn't do it, so I felt I *had* to! Then, Leonard and I put our heads together and decided to send him to the Keys at the end of summer. He said he would prefer Key West to Marathon. Actually, he didn't want to leave at all, but there was no choice. He certainly couldn't take another winter in New England.

He said he had friends in Florida, but I agonized if they could be of help. I doubted he'd tell them he had AIDS. He admitted he never even told Emory or his mother.

We gave a farewell party for Collin in October. Kay came out from California, where she was getting her MBA. Mark was here, of course, with his fiancée. A handful of our theater friends, who would be sorry to see Collin leave, came up from New York. They treated him with deference, shaking his hand and wishing him *bon voyage*. The phrase pleased him. It was the first time that day he grinned. *"Merci,"* he replied. Mark drew him aside. ⟿

COLLIN: I guess you've heard. I'm retiring.

MARK: I think it's great.

COLLIN: I don't really want to go. They're sending me away. The lady's kicking me out.

MARK: Mom wants to see you comfortable. She said you were sick. It'll be nice for you in the South. Better winters. Don't worry, I'll be down to see you, Collin. We all will. You know how often we come down to Marathon. Key West isn't far. It should be fun … only yourself to please every day. I really appreciate all you've done for me and the family. Take care, Buddy. (*He hugs* Collin *and returns to the others.*)

KAY: (*comes up*) You're awfully quiet, Collin. I've been working with AIDS patients. I hope you're not too upset that I knew.

COLLIN: Your mother has a hell of a nerve. She shouldn't have told you. She shouldn't have told anyone. I'll never forgive her!

KAY: (*smiles*) You always say that, but then you end up forgiving all of us for everything. That's the way it *should* be. Well, I forgive you, too.

COLLIN: (*surprised*) For what?

KAY: Who can remember? But I do care about you, Collin. The AIDS support groups in California are doing a wonderful job. If you get sick of the Keys, you can call me and come on out. They have parties and everything. You'd enjoy yourself. Just think. Now you'll be able to do all the reading you said you never had time for.

COLLIN: (*looking around*) I'm going to miss my garden. Miss working in it. Reading ... that's something old people do. I might as well say, as you've been told, / I won't live long enough to be old.

KAY: I'm glad you're still making those corny rhymes. Don't be morose, Collin. Life has a lot of surprises. I'll visit. We love you, Collin.

↶ He didn't answer. He wandered off to stand with the dogs near the vegetable garden he had enlarged that spring. Suddenly, he stooped, picked up Ophelia, and hugged her fiercely to his chest. She licked him and he carefully put her down, laughing as she ran in circles around his neat rows of tomato plants.

I couldn't bear to watch. I embraced Kay as she returned to our circle of friends.

A week later, I told Leonard that Collin believed himself invisible. Well, now this invisible man had a very visible disease, and couldn't face it. He'd probably ignore his friends in the Keys when he got sicker. But a support group could help him there. ◡

(Leonard *and* Jerry *enter. They join* Blair, *who was talking with* Dr. Sherman.)

BLAIR: Leonard, remember how you wanted to keep this all hushed up?

LEONARD: I don't feel that way anymore. I'll do whatever Collin needs. (*to* Jerry) What happened was that Blair introduced me to you, Jerry. I think you're really amazing, offering to come down to the Keys with us to get Collin settled. It was beyond the call of duty, since you've been in mourning such a short time.

JERRY: It's easier when you don't have to face strangers alone. Hard for me, though. Who knows when I'll need the kindness of strangers?

DR. SHERMAN: What brought you around, Mr. Stewart? Making these decisions is hard on the bystanders.

LEONARD: Let me try to shed some light on the process that followed our decision to take Collin to Key West. Well— Blair, Jerry and I boarded our plane with Collin. Collin was fifty-one that week. It would be the first time he would be on his own in twenty years. That's how long we have been employing him and taking care of the details of his life. Of course, Collin believed he was taking care of us.

I felt bad watching him assemble his possessions. There were so many books and keepsakes to choose from. He stood there for hours, packing and repacking. I will always associate him with masses of boxes in every corner of his room. Finally, he packed up a whole lifetime in six miserable boxes.

In Key West, Blair and I were told that all the personal care and attention for AIDS patients existed solely because of the Gay Men's Crisis Center. I had the idea that the evenings in Key West offered illusion, and days were carefree, so that Collin would be happy. That proved not to be the case.

BLAIR: You're so long-winded, Leonard.

DR. SHERMAN: Let him have his say, Blair. This is hard on him, too. You talked to Jerry?

LEONARD: Yes, Jerry and I spoke before we left for the Keys. We were told by Abra Simmons, the administrator of AIDS Help, that she would see us as soon as we had settled Collin's rental. When we got to Florida, Collin went straight to a new doctor. Jerry talked to Abra. This is how it went.

BLAIR: (*unpacking in Key West*) So what did she say?

JERRY: We have an appointment at eleven tomorrow. Abra will introduce Collin to the others in the support group. He'll need to bring his records and to set up a schedule of treatments. (*takes out a list*) Of course, we'll have to find Collin an apartment. From what I've heard, it's best if we can indicate he's lived here in Monroe County at least three years. Apparently, the town fathers are getting hostile about the influx of AIDS patients. Collin has to get a Florida driver's license and voter's registration.

BLAIR: This sounds like college! Oh, God. So much needs to be accomplished in four days. You look tired, Jerry. Does this depress you too much?

JERRY: It depresses me. So what? It's just that I felt, walking in there today, seeing some of the others … well, it felt like being in hell. (*sadly*) I've got to help as best I can; otherwise, I'll go out of my mind. Is Collin back from the doctor? How is he feeling?

BLAIR: Not bad. But Collin's energy is low.

BLAIR: (*to* Dr. Sherman) The next day, Monday, was bright. I was tense because Collin was acting inappropriately. He was almost joyous, seemingly oblivious of what we were there for. We didn't want to take Collin with us to look for an apartment, because of the lesions and scabs on his arms and legs. The real estate agents don't want AIDS patients in buildings with other renters. Abra said to me she was afraid someone would have to sign for him. It was devious, but what can you do? No one wants these men.

JERRY: I found a really nice apartment, but it was on the second floor. Soon Collin won't be able to climb stairs. He was drinking, too. I saw him take four bourbons.

BLAIR: He doesn't care to do what's healthy. He's smoking, and Dr. Walters had forbidden it. Still, he seems to enjoy eating.

LEONARD: We visited several real estate agencies, but all of them wanted to interview Collin. He was so thin and had those God-awful scabs that told the tale of his illness better than any words. Unfortunately, it was our predicament. Collin couldn't stay alone, even in Marathon, where our house was, without a decent hospital or support group.

BLAIR: I wanted to put Collin into one of the houses the state provides.

JERRY: Abra said the men in those houses were too young. His taste and theirs wouldn't gel. For example, what kind of music does Collin like?

LEONARD: Elevator music. Why?

JERRY: That proves her point. They like hard rock. Collin would go crazy.

BLAIR: What about visiting-nurse services? Or hospitals?

JERRY: (*gently*) The way it was with my friend—well, Collin will probably die in his apartment. Unless they start letting AIDS patients into more of the nursing homes that ban them now. It's a shame. (*sighs*) Still, the group will attend to him somehow.

LEONARD: (*to* Dr. Sherman) We did the best we could. We found a modest real estate agency on Truman Avenue with a small apartment on the ground floor in Old Town. The landlord was absentee. We could sign for Collin.

BLAIR: I thought that was unethical. Leonard, *you're* a landlord. How would you feel having one of your tenants sign a lease for someone who has AIDS? You'd be furious.

LEONARD: Legally, I don't think anyone can deny a sick person the right to live in the building. I said I was taking the apartment but wanted to put my houseman on the lease, as he would be staying there, getting it ready for me. I wasn't a bit ashamed.

BLAIR: Actually, I was thrilled with what you did and the way you did it, Len. How many people would go out of their way, the way you have for Collin? I'm so overcome, it makes me teary.

LEONARD: (*He opens his arms. She goes to him and hugs him tight.*) We'll get through this, don't you worry.

DR. SHERMAN: Yes, I think you will. The only one who won't is … Collin. (*exits*)

Entry Twenty-Five

⌐ After we found an apartment, there was more red tape. We had to take Collin to sign a power of attorney. Also, Leonard visited the local funeral parlor to make decisions that would be more difficult later. ⌐

(Blair *and* Jerry *confer.* Leonard *enters and joins them.*)

LEONARD: I felt horrible hearing the nightmarish details. I had lived with Collin so long, his symptoms were my symptoms. The only thing I didn't catch on this trip was his attitude of indifference. He seemed to have set his smile in cement. He had a vague, almost clownish expression. He seemed to be oblivious to our running around on his behalf. But I could understand that. I mean, who wants to contemplate his own demise?

Wednesday, Collin acted poorly at his first support group meeting and bragged about his use of drugs. He told the others he had free-based. Later, it occurred to me that perhaps this was a cover. If people thought he did drugs, then they wouldn't relate his AIDS to homosexuality. I had another shocker to report. It would cost two hundred extra at the funeral home to deal with an infectious disease. God, Collin would have cringed!

(Jerry *himself cringes.*)

BLAIR: It sounds so undignified. Oh Leonard, Collin has the pride of a gentleman and is far better educated in some ways than most. He loves being around beautiful things. It breaks my heart. The mortician is talking about treating his corpse as unclean? He must never know this.

LEONARD: How did he ever become such a victim?

JERRY: Drop that word, Leonard. Sorry. It's just ... we don't refer to people with AIDS as victims. They are patients.

BLAIR: After dinner, I put on a gaiety I didn't feel. I told Collin we had found a terrific apartment, right in the center of town.

(Collin *enters.*)

Guess what, Collin? We found you a wonderful place. Three bright rooms. Wait till you see it. You'll adore it!

COLLIN: (*waves it off*) Can we go dancing at the Strand?

BLAIR: Of course.

Later that evening we took him over to see the apartment.

(Collin *slowly walks around, investigating the rooms. He holds his pipe and looks pleased. He opens the closets, curious about every little thing.*)

I felt like a mother sending her child off to summer camp.

Was he going to be all right? Would he make new friends? What if … (*swallows*) he wakes up sick in the night and I'm not there? I watched Collin inspect his new home, a man with his first private castle at age fifty-one.

COLLIN: (*joins her*) I'd prefer a radio to a TV, if I have a choice.

LEONARD: You can have both. I know you love the radio. We're giving you the Marathon car to use. Take whatever you need from the house. Maybe some tapes.

BLAIR: Plants, too. There are plenty of those down here.

COLLIN: Sure. (*warming to the idea*) Maybe I could even ride your bike, Leonard. The new one?

LEONARD: Of course.

COLLIN: I can drive around, maybe go up and see the sunset from the porch in Marathon. My favorite time of day. I photograph them all the time. (*to* Blair) Remember the one I had framed for you? It's on your bureau.

BLAIR: I love that picture, Collin. I hope you'll take more.

(Collin *tests the chair. He gets up and looks around. He is examining the deck outside his rooms and the small back entrance. He comes back inside, looking depressed.*)

COLLIN: Nice wicker. But not as nice as the antique wicker we had in Falls Village. (*gesturing outside*) There's no sunlight. Not even enough to grow tomatoes or dahlias.

BLAIR: (*thinks fast*) You could grow orchids.

COLLIN: (*brightens*) Yes, I could do that. (*speculatively*) The rooms are small … still … there are three of them … like my quarters in the first Greenwich house. Could I invite my mother down?

BLAIR: (*relieved*) Of *course* you can! Bring whoever you please. I mean, it's your apartment.

COLLIN: (*mumbles*) If Mother comes ... I can always sleep on the floor. I did on the Left Bank, once. (*exits*)

↜ The next day we went to Sears and bought what he needed. We drove up to Marathon to take his money out of the bank that afternoon. The AIDS Help group suggested we do that, in order to apply for disability from Social Security. It was certainly due him, but we thought it best that he have no bank account and owned nothing. We had had to do the same with Leonard's mother when she needed full Medicaid benefits. ↜

LEONARD: When I left the bank, remember, I insisted Collin fill out a will. I brought down a blank form. Collin balked.

COLLIN: (*He enters* and *joins* Leonard at *the table. Speaks emphatically.*) I don't want to do this now!

LEONARD: You have to! Damn it, Collin, we're trying to make your responsibilities minimal, and you procrastinate. We all have wills. You should have had one years ago. Now is the time, Collin.

COLLIN: (*stubbornly*) I like to procrastinate. I like to do things gradually.

Entry Twenty-Six

↞ Leonard and I were alone. Things were deadly quiet, docile. The children were on their own, and Collin was gone. The air in the house was fresh. No pipe tobacco stinking up the kitchen at dinnertime. If I didn't pay too much attention to the mirror, to the lines around my mouth and between my eyes and didn't look down and see the slight bulge around my middle, I felt as seductive a package as I was when I was young, and Leonard and I were by ourselves in our childless apartment.

When I look at the material in my journal about our move twenty years ago to Falls Village, I see now why I felt that if a woman really wanted to kill her ambition to achieve in a big way, all she had to do was to get married. I would have told that to any young hopeful who asked me. I might feel the same way if I married these days, because there are still wandering husbands and children to be managed and men's careers to be reckoned with as well as your own. Now, in the mid nineties, it is still a dilemma. Take your career and run with it or help him run with his; a man's career or your own. My daughter tells me

LEONARD: Look! Sign it now! You can change it next week … every week, if you want to. Leave everything to your mother. Who else is there? Just sign it, Collin, and be done with it. It proved just as difficult to get you to sign the power of attorney. Surely you realize WE don't want your money. It's just that someone has to be responsible.

COLLIN: (*reluctantly*) I know it. (*signs*)

(*Scene shifts to restaurant. Blair, Jerry, Collin and* Leonard *are seated. A young* Waitress *comes over, a pad and pencil in her hands.*)

WAITRESS: I heard you say you're on your way to Key West. Wanna hear a joke? (*covers her mouth, tittering*) You won't have any trouble finding your way in Key West. You want to know why?

LEONARD: Why?

WAITRESS: Because there's AIDS on every corner—get it?

LEONARD: (*takes the girl by the arm*) You better watch that mouth of yours.

WAITRESS: Stop pulling me. What for?

LEONARD: Your humor is in bad taste. That's not funny.

WAITRESS: Well, *pardon* me. (*leaves for kitchen*)

LEONARD: You're lucky I'm not telling your boss. (*to* Collin, Blair *and* Jerry) But what can I expect? Thousands of people would think that's funny.

↞ On our last full day in Key West, Collin passed his Florida driver's test. He waved his signed voter's registration as he joined us. All small victories counted.

He smiled a lot that afternoon. He had long since forgotten the waitress' slur. Like the tea party twenty years ago, when our perceptions sailed past each other like two ships on a calm sea, he simply couldn't focus on the slight. Too much else was on his mind.

That last morning, we helped him pack the food in the refrigerator in our motel and brought it over to his apartment. His bed was neatly made, the phone was working and our station wagon was parked outside. Later that day, Collin would drive to Marathon to borrow a few paintings and *tsatskes* to make his apartment homey.

I left him my shampoo, the expensive kind he liked. He was just as vain about making his hair appear thicker as I. We gave him severance pay, a retirement gift, plus his rental and his medical insurance. He deserved it. ∽

BLAIR: We're leaving now, Collin. Jerry's packed and waiting at the plane. You're all settled now. We'll be down to visit. I won't say we'll miss you. You know that … Damn! (*looking around, not able to face him*) Where's my hat? The wide-brimmed green one. I've lost my hat, as usual.

COLLIN: I know where it is. You were carrying that hat inside my new apartment. That's the one we bought at the craft show, remember? I'll find it! (*exits*)

BLAIR: (*calls after him*) You don't have to. You no

longer … Oh, damn, double damn.

(Collin *returns, grinning from ear to ear, and hands th* her.)

COLLIN: You're always losing things, Lady.

BLAIR: Collin, for once, don't call me Lady. Call m

COLLIN: Aha! Finally caught on! You *said* don't Lady, but you never said *what* to call you. You never said, "Call me Blair." It's impolite to call a lady by her fi … unless she asks.

BLAIR: Blair, then. Please call me Blair.

COLLIN: Blair … Neville … Stewart. (*shyly*) Th The *lady*. How she huffs and puffs and sometimes glar so, she's in my prayers. (*Looks down at his hands. The out his hand to shake hers. They hug. They look away, tries to keep control.*)

COLLIN: Bye, Blair. Bye, Leonard.

LEONARD: Goodbye, Collin. We'll be down at C

BLAIR: I can't bear goodbyes. It's just for a months. We'll be back.

(*They watch as* Collin, *lighting a pipe, looks off t ocean.*)

COLLIN: I'm going down to the pier. I'll bet ther terrific sunset tonight. After the sun goes down, e claps. (*He smiles and exits. The lights fade.*)

women should "do" for themselves first. Well, I didn't *dare* feel that way then.

I could honestly say that I was a far cry from the young, dark, intense actress who strutted the stage so proud and self-assured in *Girl on the Via Flaminia*. I didn't look bad. Like Mother, I was olive-skinned. "Mediterranean coloring," some called it. The good news was that some people mentioned that I had a certain grace and elegance. I didn't know about that. I'd be lying if I didn't admit I still felt pretty enough. Bone structure will out, Collin always said. I could see I was still attractive by the way men looked at me at parties. The bad news was that my voice was a bit excitable. Even my friends said that. Perhaps I could best describe myself as a vivacious brunette with a flair for the dramatic. A type-A personality, as they say in pop-psychology books, prone to jealousy. "Animated," Leonard called me. That was probably why he married me in the first place. He always swore that he loved unpredictable women: women who surprised him. I tried to keep up that particular expectation.

Let me bring Leonard onto the scene and write how he looked to me.

In his fifties, Leonard still had the shadow of freckles on his cheeks. He was wiser than he once was. His sense of morality had finally developed. His hair was still sandy, but a bit gray. He was more attractive than ever. His smile was gregarious and teasing still. He didn't chase women, although flirtatiousness would always be a part of his modus operandi. There would always be a Muffy or a Bambi hanging around wistfully. His friends liked him better. It was probably because he didn't brag as much. He reminded me of a sturdy bear and I liked him that way; I'm glad he was no longer the slender rake I loved and married. Lucky, because I no longer had the energy to put up with his immaturity. Or maybe it was just that I thought better of myself, so he thought better of me.

Almost six months went by. Spring was returning. For a while, Leonard and I in Connecticut and Collin in the Keys managed in our separate spheres. Gradually, guilt and loneliness crept in as insidiously as night followed one of Collin's sunsets. A few weeks after his arrival in Key West, his first letter came. I didn't know why I wasn't hearing from him more regularly. He sounded abrupt on the phone.

Now this becomes Collin's story, more than ever. Therefore, I will let him narrate it as he did in his letters to me ... letters that told of his bitterness, his sense of abandonment and his rage. ⮌

(Collin *enters*. Blair *hands him his letter, which he reads aloud*.)

COLLIN: This is *my* entry, *my* voice, as Blair hears it. (*reads*) Dear Blair and Leonard. I came here to this sappy little apartment in Key West under protest. I was used to much nicer, living with you. I'll admit I'm spoiled. Whatever ...

It seems to be the best place. They've been concerned in every way. In Key West, there were too many "hangers on" and the clouded drug scene, in and out of reality—too many times. Most of my early letters were so negative that I trashed them. Since the latter part of February, the depression part of this so-called illness has gotten me down. It makes me tired, with no energy.

I've been a real loner with no plans for the future and not much to look forward to except to change my so-called will, with which I'm not at all happy. There is so little, I want to put it on my burial.

I've built up a great deal of anger and even hate toward Dr. Walters and the others at the hospital. None of them observed any sense of decency and privacy that one has a right to, regardless of the nature of one's illness. Violating my request that EMPHATICALLY NO ONE BE TOLD OF MY SICKNESS. Emory said when he called, *you* told him! How could you? I suppose you're going to say moral responsibility, but who cares about that? Your gossiping has bothered me. You probably told others as well! I wanted it to be kept private, so now how about retracting your various statements by telling everyone you were wrong, that medical evidence is not conclusive? Otherwise, I can never come north again.

Excuse miss-spelling—I have no dictionary; a few hundred or more books are scattered about in Connecticut, along with clothes and other personal items I've taken years to collect. It has been bothering me more and more, as time has gone on. When I start to look for something, it's like only part of me is here. I'll bet you threw my stuff out! Well, I can't prove that.

Sure, there are times I'm lonely. I do miss the dogs as they're fun and so loyal. More so than people.

It's difficult for me to communicate my real feelings with the anger about life and my health and no future, except for my demise in some months. A couple of men have passed on in recent weeks and I've noted the deterioration. It bums me out.

I worked on two sets at the Fine Arts Center. One was *Oh Coward.* They didn't know I'm a theater connoisseur, thanks to you. Their lighting designer stunk.

They had a cabaret evening as a benefit for AIDS Help one night at the Tennessee Williams Theater. The lighting was good on that one. There was an actress in it who wasn't half as good as you.

This afternoon I'll go over to see what I can do to work at the new offices for AIDS Help. It's hard to get there, since the police took my car (your car). Yes, I was arrested for selling drugs. I suppose Abra told you that. I have to take the bus to the doctor and the support group. You know I hate busses.

I've given some thought about what has happened in my life the past few months, especially with my health. I would prefer to be well and working every day. I'm not happy with my ups and downs. I guess I have to admit it, I do miss quite a few people and the gardening and the lifestyle I had. I miss planning trips. Right now, I even miss going up to Marathon a couple of times a month. Unless I see some improvement in all phases of my life and get off everyone's blacklist, I foresee the end of my life in a few months. I'm aware of my failures, of which there have been quite a few. I tried my best, most of the time. Now I'm tired, depressed and want to give up.

I hate the guys from the cruise ships hanging out at my pad, I hate coping with the hot sun. I sleep a lot. Am getting weaker. Somehow, I really just don't care anymore even to pay my electric.

Two days later.

Tonight it's beautiful, with almost a full moon. It's called the paschal moon, the one just before Easter. Remember when I told you nature was important? Well, it's not just important, it's *everything*. Every time I see flowers, I think of Falls Village and crocuses in the spring. So yellow. So beautiful.

So far, no special plans, except church.

Blair, your cross-country adventure sounds real interesting, and I admit a certain envy. I used to enjoy the drives back and forth to the Keys, and I also feel fortunate having done some driving across part of this vast country of ours. Anyhow, it sounds like you're having a fulfilling life, going where you wish and doing things you enjoy. It's great that you and Leonard are finally having a good time together. It was wonderful hearing from you, Blair.

Please forgive my negativity. Give the two dogs my love. I hope that if things change for the better, I might reverse my feelings and be able to write more positively. Take care and all that. (Collin *gives* Blair *back the letter and exits.*)

⮌ I retreated into my journal. Time went by. Every day, all day, Collin was on my mind. I couldn't look at flowers or a sunset without thinking of how he loved these things. Collin's departure created a big, fat void in our family. I didn't know how the children felt, off in their own worlds, but I didn't feel well those days. A vague sort of pain persisted. As usual, the pain I felt was in the wrong place: dislocated. Anxiety made my body hurt. Guilt, no doubt, caused it. A backlash of all that had happened.

Yes, the pain of Collin's departure created an ache that wouldn't go away. I was the one, think of it, who finally said goodbye. He didn't leave on his own accord. I had to retire him, because I couldn't cope any longer. Leonard could never handle goodbyes. That's probably why we're still married.

Those months Collin was in the Keys, he was all mixed up on how he felt about us. At Christmas we came by, and he wouldn't let us in. The Key West scene *was* a mess. The neighbors complained. Said he was mixed up with selling drugs and insisted AIDS Help evict him. Then we got a call from the pharmaceutical firm, reporting that they had sent him medication and were never paid. We traced the payment through Medicare. A check for ten thousand dollars went to Collin. A sailor stole it, or so Collin said. Shortly after that, AIDS Help called and said they had found him half dead in his apartment. He hadn't paid the electric bill, had no food: in short, he wanted to die. They took him to the hospital. After that, they found him lodgings in a convalescent home right near our place in

Marathon. Providential. He sprang back to life. He was delight-ed that it had the same view he had enjoyed for years, out over the flats of Bonefish Harbor. ⌐

BLAIR: (*writes*) A letter just arrived from you, Collin. Thank heaven you're writing to me now—long letters, so I don't feel as bad. You know the power of purging as well as I. What cruel accusations you hurled at us! Those were angry let-ters. The time of dissembling was over. In all the years I acted on stage and whenever else possible, never have I needed to use my talent to dissemble as much as I did when dealing with you.

When I picked up the mail this morning, there was your lat-est letter. That will make three in all, over the last eight months. Collin, don't be so furious and destructive down in Florida, doing whatever you're doing. You need to forgive and have courage. ⌐

(Collin *enters. He motions to her to let him speak again. She nods and hands him another letter. He reads aloud.*)

COLLIN: So much has happened. I hope this letter is more optimistic for you. I hate to always be writing in a funk. But how else should I be? Dear Blair and Leonard—How's every-one and how are things going? Let's hope okay.

You were right, what you said in your journal. Right about how things went for me in Key West. I was at the doorway of the next life. I was good and frightened. I've replaced some of the clothes my friends stole, but it's a rough game.

I can't believe it! No one but you wrote me. The convalescent home is so boring after the Stewart menagerie.

BLAIR: (*breaks into* Collin's *reading of the letter*) Why are you surprised? If *you* don't write anyone, how can you expect them to write? You said to tell no one where you were. Besides, if anyone knew what you were up to, they wouldn't want to write. (*disgusted*) Getting busted for drugs! You sure turned into a wild one. Letting it all hang out, or getting a little revenge on the world? We didn't even know if you were alive down there in Key West.

COLLIN: (*puts letter aside*) The drug bust was a frame. Now I bet you'll think I stole your jewelry years ago, but that was really that friend of Mark's, that Jeffry Something-or-other. Don't try to hang that one on me.

When Emory was in Key West with me ... I was pushing then. The thing is, the police just got around to picking everyone up. What difference did it make? They wouldn't keep me in jail. They admitted that when they let me out. Then I was on the streets. That's when somebody called AIDS Help, and they got me into the home in Marathon.

BLAIR: Why wouldn't they keep you in jail?

COLLIN: They don't know how to deal with AIDS in jails. They wouldn't even consider putting me there for more than one night. The others? They're in. Not me. Emory's in St. Louis, so they couldn't touch him. I just got probation. I can do whatever I like now.

BLAIR: (*ironically*) That's comforting. Bet you could get

away with murder, knowing the police won't incarcerate you. Well, you nearly died in Key West, so they took you to the hospital and then you got out and got arrested. Why did you screw up?

COLLIN: A last fling, I suppose. Yeah, I'm tired. It's nice here in the convalescent home. I have my own room and the food's not too bad. At least there's air conditioning. There's an Episcopal minister who takes me to church on Sundays. He comes and talks, too. Yeah, I'm going to behave myself from here on.

BLAIR: Good for you, Collin. How did they take care of you in the hospital?

COLLIN: (*reads from the letter again*) There were only two or three doctors who were interested, but the nurses and aides gave me good care. I guess I tried to die. They were at me a couple of days to wake up and live. Now some of them are friends.

It was the loneliness. That's why I turned to people who helped me escape. Here, I'm the happiest I've been in years. Besides the minister, I'm visited by the local baker, who used to sell us those Florida-imitation bagels. I eat as much as I can now. I have no desire to do drugs. Ever! I have no idea how numbered my days are, but I plan to enjoy myself in simple ways.

I feel bad about people doing things for me, but I have limits to how I can repay them. All my possessions are gone. It's twenty-one years lost and down the drain. That really hurts.

But I *do* know I'm responsible, to a degree. Anyway, I appreciate your nice letters. I hope both of you, and anyone else who remembers me, will visit. I'm keeping my life in order. Blair, you'd enjoy it here. A lot of good stories. It's so great to have a clear mind, not clouded or fogged up from cocaine. I don't want to lead a dual life any longer. You'll notice the change the next time you come down. Karen Baker is my social worker. She wants to meet you, Blair. She is a beautiful girl, too.

I still need to get a dictionary. Not a big one, just for everyday use.

I shall close for now and hope I can see everyone again. Thank you both for being part of my life. Please, my genuine love to all. Especially Ophelia.

Love, Collin.

(Collin *folds the letter. He walks to the right of the table and sits, filling his pipe, tamping it down.* Joanie *enters. She doesn't see him.*)

⮌ I've decided, at this point, to bring Joanie back into my journal, because she just showed up one day as if nothing had happened. About the time she reentered my life, I really needed her and was glad. ⮌

BLAIR: (*to* Joanie) Hello there, stranger. How's your love life?

JOANIE: The same as ever, convoluted. Well, Blair, I'm back. It took a while, but I got here. I feel bad for what I said to the support group. I feel worse about Collin. He sent me a lovely Easter card. He even wrote his own rhyme. "Whatever happened to my pal, / the girl with flare, the *femme fatale?*" That made me cry. Is there something I can do for him?

BLAIR: Welcome back, Joanie. I have to hand it to you, I never thought you'd have the nerve to show your face to us. I know Collin would love to hear from you. Mostly, he needs visitors. But I suppose that's asking too much.

JOANIE: I'm sorry your friend John died. So young. How's Bill?

BLAIR: Devastated. Don't sympathize, if you don't really mean it.

JOANIE: I *do. I* want to phone Collin right now. Dial his number. I'm not wearing my glasses.

(*Phone rings.* Collin *picks up the receiver, holding his pipe in the other hand.*)

COLLIN: (*taking a puff*) Hello, Collin Williams here. Who may I ask is calling?

JOANIE: Collin, it's Joan Landau. Thanks for the Easter card. It made me remember good times.

COLLIN: (*preening, filled with pride*) That's music to my ears, Joanie. Glad to hear from you. The Stewarts will be down one of these days. You wouldn't happen to be coming with them, would you? Because if you are ... I'd love to see you once more.

JOANIE: (*She pauses, thinks, makes a decision, looks at* Blair *and nods.*) It so happens, I'm driving down next week. Scuba diving with a new beau. I'd adore seeing you.

COLLIN: That's wonderful!

JOANIE: Can you possibly suggest the best route?

COLLIN: (*puffing on his pipe*) Just a minute. I have a new map right here. (*beaming*) Have you a pad and pencil? You know how to get to the Jersey Turnpike from the Garden State? Okay, take the turnpike to I-95 South. Now it gets tricky. Those crazy daisy loops outside Washington. (*The lights fade slowly.*) Keep on I-95 to Jacksonville and switch over to 255. Then pick up 95 again and stay on until Miami. From Miami, you take US-1. There's one thing I have yet to say, / Beware US-1, the widow maker's highway. But you don't have to worry; you're not married right now.

JOANIE: Very funny, Collin. I see you haven't changed.

COLLIN: The more you change, the more you remain the same. I read that someplace. Drive carefully. The cops are heavy once you hit Florida. And watch out, driving near Miami. Then US-1 goes straight as an arrow, all the way to Marathon.

↩ This is near the end of my journal. I want to be sure Collin has the last scene, even if I have the final words. Collin's strange innocence didn't keep him safe. He was filled with so much anxiety. If only he had understood how to take care of himself! In short, understood how to love himself. I've begun to see, lately, that *all* diseases, the real ones and the ones in our minds, might have been brought on by lack of faith in ourselves and in others. It was certainly true of my jealousy—a lack of faith in myself. I'm beginning to understand that and am trying to trust everyone important to me.

We care so much what people think of us. It's really very stupid … But guilt is guilt and our own reputation is still one of the most important things in the world to us. We suffer so about how others perceive us, at least Collin did. All his life he did.

It appalled me the way Collin perceived his illness. I hated to think that sick people saw their dysfunctions as being either "respectable" or "unrespectable," and *that* perception can put a taint on life that is more painful than illness. The bad names we call ourselves never wash off.

So, I should do what Collin wanted … tell people he was dying of cancer or pneumonia, help Collin hide his life, just as he did when he used to hide from our guests to pretend he didn't prepare the meal, that he wasn't in the domestic-help category.

But even before we took him to Florida, people saw him getting sicker and sicker. They knew, I'm sure. I could have denied it. I could have said anything. But I doubt many would have believed me.

It bothers me that some might think of his lifestyle as tawdry. I just can't believe God condemns us for something as trivial as our sexual responses. No, I never thought what he did sexually was against nature. I don't think God gave Collin AIDS to punish him. Not because he took drugs or because he was attracted to men.

The drugs? No, I didn't like it that he did them in our house. That our children might have been influenced. I mean, the children got into marijuana awfully early, and I hope it wasn't Collin's example. I did sometimes think what went on in those despicable rooms of his was dark and unpleasant. I do know he was a lonely man who tried to buy friends. So many of us do. If not with drugs, with dinners and parties and whatever the affluent have at their convenience. The only part of it all that I feel is immoral is the rumor that Collin slept around in Key West and didn't tell his partners that he had AIDS. That I find despicable. Of course, it was only a rumor. But then, knowing Collin and his streak of spitefulness, it could have been true. I always hated the deceptive side of Collin's nature, just as I hated the deceptive side of Leonard's.

There is no pat or ideal resolution to living. That is my message. That is what I felt was important enough to write about in the first place. We live as best we can, while we can. Now I'm closing my computer. I'm finished. My journal-play-story is complete, my questioning over. Blackout. ༄

Epitaph

⤶ A month ago Collin died. He had written how kind the minister and Mike, the baker, were. Collin said he loved the attention of decent people. He wrote that the convalescent home was boring, so we sent him on a weekend cruise while his strength still held. All he had to do was take a bus up to Miami. The cruise was what they called "A Trip to Nowhere."

It seemed only weeks before his death that Leonard and I had gone down to the Keys for a visit and some relaxation in Marathon. The harbor was alive with boats returning from fishing. The sun was shining. People trailed past our house on the way to the beach. Those were days for walking.

Collin's convalescent home was less than a quarter-mile from our house. I had suggested to him that it would make a perfect afternoon walk, but he said his legs were bothering him and he had given up walks. He also said he had laundry to do. That he didn't like the way the laundry was handled at the home and wanted to bring it to our house. I realized that meant I would be the one elected to iron, unless he had given up the habit of ironing his jeans. Heaven knew what his prerogatives were these days!

When I picked him up at the home, the first thing I noticed was that he was frighteningly thin. ↫

BLAIR: How wonderful to see you, Collin. You look rested.

COLLIN: (*beaming*) Glad to see you. Come on, I want to get out of here. The only time I get out is to go to church. I can't wait to see our house.

(Blair *leads him downstairs, carrying his laundry in a K-Mart bag.*)

BLAIR: Get in, Collin. I'll put your things in the back seat.

COLLIN: See you got the car back. What'd you do, paint it white? I liked it better beige. Classier. White cars look like old-fashioned refrigerators.

BLAIR: I'll fix lunch when we get home. You need anything from the store, first?

COLLIN: Just some pipe tobacco, if you don't mind. And some Q-tips for my ears. A little film, too. I want to take a picture of Karen Baker. That social worker I wrote you about.

↫ We swung by the pharmacy for his tobacco and then I pulled in front of Pantry Pride. Collin, businesslike, handed me a list of special cookies and cereals he liked. Dutifully, I went in, while he waited in the air-conditioned car. I got him what he wanted. It would have been easy, except that lines at the market are always long. When I got back to the car, I noticed with alarm that his face was very flushed and he looked worse than before. I also saw that he had a cut on his cheek, probably from shaving. I reminded myself to ask him to wash it off before he kissed or hugged anybody else.

The cool breeze was more pronounced as we headed into our driveway. Collin got out of the car and looked at the ocean with a serenity that made me glad we had come down. He stood for a moment, holding on to the banister on his way up to the covered porch, while I carried in his groceries to refrigerate them until we returned to the convalescent home. Then I went back for his laundry. ⌒

BLAIR: Go on up, Collin. Take your time. I know you can't wait to stretch out on the chaise and stare out at the ocean. When I'm in Connecticut, that's how I always think of you.

COLLIN: I've been dreaming about this porch. I've missed looking out at the sandbar, the ships in the Gulf Stream. I always worry about freighters spilling oil.

BLAIR: Don't you have a porch at Marathon Manor that looks out at the water? There's a beach in front.

COLLIN: It's been too hot. I really can't stay in the sun. No, there's no porch. My room faces the back. I've been sort of low, anyway. I don't want to go out much.

(*They walk slowly up the stairs.* Blair *holds back;* Collin *seems very tired.*)

BLAIR: What do you do all day?

COLLIN: Listen to music. Watch television, mostly. I have basic cable. Thanks for treating me to that. I'm grateful for the checks you send. They keep me going. (*pauses*) Anyway, I love the old Bogart films. I saw Ron Randall in one of his early pictures, too. (*sheepishly*) I thought of the play you did with him. Hey, I'm getting really hungry!

(Leonard *comes to the screened-porch door and opens it for* Collin.)

LEONARD: Hey, fella. Good to see you. Give us a hug!

BLAIR: (*quickly*) Collin's hot and sweaty, Honey. We've just been shopping. You want to wash up, first? Oh, look, Collin. You've got a little blood on your cheek. Must have been from shaving. Maybe you want to wash it off before you get Leonard all messy.

COLLIN: (*embarrassed*) Yeah, I'll be right back. Then maybe we could eat?

(Collin *goes into the bathroom.*)

BLAIR: Leonard, be careful what you touch of his! Come on, I'll fix his lunch. You go on down and put his clothes into the washing machine. That way they'll be ready when he leaves.

LEONARD: (*amused*) Are you going to iron them, too?

BLAIR: (*whispers*) He ironed for us for twenty years. He took care of *me.* I guess the shoe is on the other foot.

LEONARD: You're a good scout, Blair. (*calls to* Collin) Hurry, Collin. We have a lot of catching up to do.

⌢ Leonard did the wash while Collin sat on the porch, staring at the sea as if it would disappear if he were to look away. ⌢

COLLIN: (*calls into the kitchen*) What are you making?

BLAIR: Tuna fish, lettuce and tomato salad, all right? It's what *we're* having.

COLLIN: I'd prefer an omelet. They make terrible egg dishes at the Manor. Mrs. Eldridge down the hall is always complaining. You'd like her. She knits a kind of slipper for me, like a kid's bootie. She tells me a lot of stories. She won't touch their eggs, and neither will I. Listen, could I have a cup of coffee with milk and plenty of sugar?

BLAIR: (*She enters, placing a tray before* Collin, *who inspects the contents of his coffee cup.*) So, what do you want to know about what's happening back north? I've got all sorts of news.

COLLIN: Excuse me a minute, Blair. Before we get into a long conversation, could I have a little more coffee? You know I like it filled to the top. Maybe you could bring the pot and leave it out here.

BLAIR: Anything else?

COLLIN: (*grins*) What's for dessert?

BLAIR: There's nothing in the house, Collin. You know we're always dieting.

COLLIN: (*eating enthusiastically*) It doesn't matter. Maybe we could get some Key Lime pie at the Cracked Conch on our way back. Do you think while you're here, you could bring me some homemade brownies?

↬ Nothing had changed. I was cooking for Collin, not what I wanted, but what he wanted. I would iron his clothes and, if he changed his mind and wanted something chocolate, I'd get him that too. Why not, if it made him happy to live in the manner to which we had made him accustomed? He was an individual partly of my own creation.

But that was a few months ago. In New England it was summer, and Collin's garden in Greenwich was in full bloom. I thought of him every day, when I looked at the perennials. Especially the roses and the peonies.

When we heard the bad news, Leonard and I went down to the Keys and retrieved his ashes, as Collin had requested. The funeral parlor was holding them for us. The nursing home gave everything away, including his television and my paintings. Collin had worked for eight months on the two-page document that was his last testament. His final estate amounted to not quite one hundred dollars.

Later that day, there was a hurricane alert and the wind was howling the way it sometimes does in the Keys. Kay and Mark had flown down, too. Their flights had been delayed because of storm warnings.

Around six o'clock, we decided it was time for the ceremony. I was dreading it, while wanting it to be over. I'd felt that way about Mother's funeral, as well. The tide was high and the water very choppy. A hot, stinging wind was blowing directly in our faces, as we walked out on the pier over Bonefish Flats. I carried the small cardboard box with Collin's ashes inside. Kay held the bouquet of flowers we had picked from those Collin had planted—bougainvillea and hibiscus.

BLAIR: How will I do this?

MARK: Say a prayer, Mother. An epitaph. A eulogy to Collin. He would have loved the adulation.

BLAIR: *Sh'ma Yisroel Adonoy Elohenu Adonoy Echod.* Hear O Israel, the Lord Our God, the Lord Is One. I lift up mine eyes unto the mountains, from whence cometh my help. My help cometh from the Lord who made heaven and earth. He that keepeth thee shall not slumber, he that keepeth Israel shall neither slumber nor sleep.

KAY: (*gently*) Mother, Collin wasn't Jewish. Why don't you try the Lord's Prayer?

LEONARD: And be careful when you throw the ashes. They're meant to go in the sea, not back in our faces.

KAY: Stand over here, Mother. Here are the flowers. Those should go in the water at the same time.

MARK: (*pondering*) He wanted to be buried at sea. This is dockside. We should get into the rowboat and take him farther out.

LEONARD: Don't worry, the ashes will drift out, mix with

the tide. It's the ceremony that's important. Collin would understand. He loved pomp and circumstance.

KAY: Say the prayer, Mother. It might rain.

BLAIR: (*looking at the sad, soggy box*) Rain was falling the day Collin and I met, the day I made a pact with the devil. Collin was his part of the bargain.

MARK: So what was your part?

LEONARD: Her immortal soul.

BLAIR: Oy!

KAY: Stop fooling around. This is about Collin. (*starts to cry*) Let me say something.

LEONARD: Go ahead, Honey.

KAY: Collin, you were good to us. I don't know what Mother and Daddy would have done without you. Twenty years is a long time. I know we'll never forget you. Collin, you had some mouth on you! And you made terrible rhymes. But you were a part of our lives. It was a shame we couldn't have been with you more often during these terrible, final weeks. I'm sure you were very brave. Goodbye, Collin. *Bon voyage.*

LEONARD: *Bon voyage!*

MARK: And *bonne chance!*

BLAIR: *Au revoir,* Collin.

LEONARD: Go on, Blair, throw them. Now's the time. Say something first, then do it.

BLAIR: Collin, to grieve for you is no disgrace; / (*pauses*) When I say my prayers, I see your face … The Lord is my shepherd, I shall not want. He maketh me to lie down in green pastures; he leadeth me beside still waters; he restoreth my soul.

Goodbye, Collin. Just remember, in your next incarnation, you'll be a sea captain. Just as in mine, I'll be the finest actress on the American stage.

⤻ I scattered Collin's ashes as best I could, followed by Kay's flowers. The wind distributed the ashes, the sea swallowed them. As our little group lingered, the sky grew light. Amazingly, faint bands of orange heralded a sunset. Delighted, I smiled and started to clap. Leonard and Kay joined in. ⤻

MARK: Hold it! I've got the perfect farewell, learned from the master.

(*He puts the back of his hand up to his lips and makes a noise that sounds exactly like an exuberant breaking of wind.*)

MARGOT TENNEY, author, earned television, film and theater acting credits. She has three grown children; homes in Connecticut and Florida; three little granddaughters; and one spouse. She also has on hand a few thousand pages of as-yet unpublished fiction. Her writing credits, in addition to *Dark Deeds, Sweet Songs*, are the scripts for two horror movies produced by her husband, Dell, and sold to Turner Broadcasting. Founder of the Hartman Theater, Margot Tenney spent 15 years acting, reviewing scripts and supporting theater arts in Connecticut and New York. She serves on the boards of Planned Parenthood of Connecticut, Bennington College and First Stamford Corporation. She was among those honored as outstanding during the United Nations' "Year of the Woman."

HERE'S WHAT THEY'RE SAYING ABOUT THIS BOOK:

"It is an interesting story and would definitely make a good movie for television."

—Joanne Woodward

"…I found a good deal to admire about Dark Deeds, Sweet Songs. *The writing is, for the most part, on a high level; the character of Collin is provocative in his contradictions; and I felt I had gained some insights by reading the book."*

—Ring Lardner, Jr.

"Collin lives … he really does!!"

—Bari Wood

"Margot Tenney is a gifted writer … Dark Deeds, Sweet Songs *is a riveting, theatrical, sobering and gallant personal diary of our times."*

—Alexander H. Cohen

ARGONNE PUBLISHING INC. is a nonprofit organization that publishes significant literary fiction and nonfiction by authors who have yet to publish a book. It is funded by individuals and foundations who revere the well-written word and encourage its proliferation. This is Argonne's premier selection.